Cody-
Thank you for gracing my cover!

chasin' you

TERI KAY

Teri Kay

Cover Design: Cover Lovin' Designs
Cover Models: Cassandra Lynn and Cody Smith
Cover Photographer: Melissa Deanching

About the Book:

The day *Johana Warner* started at Newport Shores Middle School, *Adam Crawford* knew his life would never be the same. Her long blonde hair and ocean-blue eyes instantly grabbed his heart.
No matter how many times he tried during their fifteen-year friendship, Johana continuously kept him in the friendzone, not willing to cross that line in fear or losing the best friend she'd ever had
Now, both are in relationships they think could be the "one". Yet life has a way of shaking up plans, throwing curveballs no one saw coming.
Will these best friends stop chasing the wrong ones or will life's path finally guide them to each other?

Also by Teri Kay:

The Cave Series:
RECKLESS ABANDON
RECKLESS BEHAVIOR
RECKLESS DESIRE
RECKLESS TIES
RECKLESS LOVE

The Full Circle Duet:
ONE-EIGHTY
THREE-SIXTY

Standalones:
*SIN*ICAL HEART

Anthologies:
STORYBOOK PUB, Volume One

Dedication:

To my beautiful cousin Jeanet:
Though we never met, you and I were kindred spirits.
We understood each other, and our friendship always had me laughing.
You were a beautiful person inside and out, who was taken from us too soon.
Thank you for being my guardian angel who reminds me
"I got this".

Chapter One

Johana

Ian was supposed to be here at five-thirty. It's now seven-fifteen, and I have yet to hear from him. I try calling, but it goes straight to voicemail; I try texting, but each message remains unread.

Should I call the hospitals?

A knock at the door stops my heart. Fear tightens a fist around my chest.

Something's happened.

My stomach sinks.

Something bad has happened to Ian. There's no way he would ditch me on my birthday unless something has happened to him.

The pounding on the door continues, but my body is frozen in place.

"It's bad. I know it's something bad," I mumble, still unable to bring myself to answer the door.

"Jo, what are you still doing here?" Kenzie rushes to answer the door.

"Hey," Adam says as he walks inside our apartment. "Are you guys ready?"

My best friend's eyes meet mine and widen, then he rushes over to me. "Joey, what's wrong?"

When I don't answer, he looks at my roommate.

"I don't know what's going on," Kenzie says. "I came downstairs for the first time all evening and Johana's still here."

"Ian hasn't shown up," I finally say. "He isn't answering his phone or his text messages. I think something's happened to him."

Adam and Kenzie sit on either side of me on the couch.

Kenzie puts her arm around my shoulders. "Sweetie, do you really think something has happened to Ian? I mean, this isn't the first time he's stood you up."

"He wouldn't stand me up on my birthday unless something was seriously wrong," I snap in defense of my boyfriend.

"I don't know," Adam says, his voice hesitant, "the guy is kind of a douchebag, Joey."

I huff. "Whatever, Adam. You've never liked anyone I've dated. And why are you even here?"

"Calm down, Jo." Kenzie cocks an eyebrow. "Adam came over to help Bella and me get an after party ready for you since Ian always has you home by eleven."

"It is weird the guy gives himself a curfew," Isabella chimes in as she heads down the stairs.

Bristling, I say, "He goes to work early."

"We *all* go to work early, Jo. Stop defending him." Kenzie motions to Adam on the other side of me. "Adam's right, the guy's a douche canoe. You can do so much better."

"You guys don't understand. I love Ian and he loves me. Yes, he can be a bit neurotic about how and when we spend time together, but it's just because he has a demanding job."

"Do you even hear yourself?" Isabella scoffs. "He's a freaking city councilman!"

"All right, everyone. Let's calm down." As usual, Adam remains calm in the face of drama.

Tears flood my eyes, despite my efforts to not cry.

Adam squeezes my thigh. "If you believe something is wrong, then we'll go look for Ian."

"He said he had something special planned tonight. I don't think he'd stand me up, would he?" I look at my friends for reassurance.

None of them look at me because none of them are willing to lie to make me feel better, even if it is my birthday.

"Let me make some phone calls," Adam offers.

As soon as he takes his phone out of his pocket, mine begins vibrating off the table.

"Ian!" I grab the phone as soon as I see his name and answer the call. "Oh my god, Ian! Are you okay? Where are you?"

"Hi, pretty girl. I'm sorry, I got stuck at work. I'm not going to be able to make it tonight."

"Seriously? It's my birthday. I thought we were going to do something special. Just come over when you're done with whatever is going on."

"I have to be back here early tomorrow." His voice is quiet and shaky.

"On a Saturday?"

"I'll make it up to you, babe. Gotta go. Love you." He hangs up before I get the chance to respond.

"He didn't even wish me a happy birthday," I say through tearful gasps.

"Two words," Kenzie says as she stands. "I'll repeat them again. Douche. Canoe. Johana, you're a gorgeous woman in the prime of her life. Stop wasting your time on these jerks." She turns to Adam. "Adam, why don't you take our birthday girl here to get something to eat while Isabella and I get ready for one kick ass party."

I shake my head before Adam can answer. "I just want to throw on some old sweats and eat ice cream."

"Oh no you don't." Isabella grabs my purse, tossing it into my lap. "Adam, take her and feed her so we can get her drunk later. We'll cry over Douche Canoe tomorrow. Tonight, we party!"

"Come on." Adam stands, then extends his hand to pull me up. "There's no arguing with Isabella. Let's go. It's your birthday. Anywhere you want, beautiful."

"I'm not hungry."

"Okay, tacos it is," Adam teases.

I place my hand in his and allow him to pull me up, then lead me to the door. My roommates follow us closely, probably making sure I can't change my mind and bolt up the stairs.

Breathing deeply, I offer them a small smile and leave our condo. I have no choice but to try and make the most of this evening.

I mean, it couldn't get any worse, could it?

The beach is unusually empty for a warm night in February. I'm definitely not complaining; the crowds will invade my little beach town soon, just like they do every summer.

"How many birthdays have we spent together?" Adam shoves a bite of his carne asada taco into his mouth.

We're settled on the sandy steps beside the pier. "You ask the same thing every year. You know exactly how many." I laugh, leaning into his shoulder.

"Fifteen birthdays."

"And you've never forgotten one. Thanks, Adam."

"That's what best friends do."

Smiling, I lean over and grab another taco from our shared plate.

A blood-curdling scream comes from the street level above. Adam's emergency room instincts kick in and he bounds up the stairs, taking them two at a time to reach the screaming woman.

Scrambling to hurry behind him without dropping our food, I race up the stairs. When I reach the top, Adam is crouched down, bracing the shoulders of a *very* pregnant woman. She lies on the ground, gripping her stomach, her face contorted by pain.

"What can I do?" I ask.

"My husband is on his way," she bites out through clenched teeth.

Adam's eyes meet mine. "Stay with her. I'm going to clear out traffic, so her husband has a place to park."

"Got it." I set the food down and settle beside her, wrapping my arm around her shoulders to offer support.

"Thank you." She takes a few short breaths. "I'm not due for another five weeks but I think she's decided to come early."

"Sometimes they do that." I offer her a sympathetic smile.

Her face pinches with a new wave of pain.

I grimace, unable to offer her anything more than my presence.

When the pain subsides again, she nods toward the parking lot. "There's my husband with the car." She moves to stand, so I help her up, standing beside her so she can lean her body against mine as she waits for her husband to get out of the car.

"Diana! I'm here."

I gasp at the sound of her husband's voice. My muscles go rigid.

Three nights ago, that voice was in my bed, begging me to do all those dirty things he likes.

Just before my knees buckle, Adam wraps his arms around my waist. "I got you," he whispers.

I raise my head and my eyes lock with Ian's. The cold detachment in his gaze sends a deep chill through my spine. He helps his wife into his BMW, then hurries to the driver's side, squealing his tires as he takes off out of the parking lot, then heads down Pacific Coast Highway.

Chapter Two

Adam

Pulling into Johana's beachfront neighborhood, the narrow streets are lined with cars packed in like sardines, one after another. Groups of people, many of which I've never seen before, are heading the same direction we are.

"Who are all these people?" she asks, like I'm supposed to know.

"Apparently, Bella thinks the best way for you to get over your broken heart is with a rager."

"She knows me well." Joey shrugs.

"Ready to party, beautiful birthday girl?" I ask, parking in her driveway.

"Ahh, you're gonna make me blush." She playfully slaps my chest.

"I just call 'em like I see 'em. Eyes as blue as the ocean, hair as golden as the sun, and an ass so perfect men would fight wars just to touch it," I pronounce in my best Shakespeare impersonation.

"You're such a dork. And I love you for it. Thank you." She smiles brightly enough to light a thousand rooms.

I gently lift her chin until her eyes meet mine. "I'd do anything to keep this smile on your face."

A loud pounding on the passenger side window startles us from our moment. Isabella's nose is smashed against Jo's window. "Let's go! There's, like, a hundred people upstairs awaiting the birthday girl's arrival." She opens Joey's door and pulls her out.

"Who are all these people?" I ask as I follow the girls through a shoulder-to-shoulder crowd of people.

"Friends, friends of friends, neighbors. Anyone I could think of to help make Jo's twenty-eighth birthday a night we will never forget. Cheers!" She hands us each a shot of some green concoction, which we drink, no questions asked. Two more follow to get the party started.

"Dance with me." Joey grabs my hand, pulling me to the living room without giving me the chance to answer.

"No one else is dancing. This isn't a high school prom." I swear she asks just because she knows how much I hate dancing.

"I don't care. It's my birthday and I want to dance." She raises one eyebrow in challenge. "You're not gonna make the birthday girl dance alone, are you?"

Frowning, I say, "Joey—"

"I'll dance with the beautiful lady, if you don't to."

I swivel my head toward the interruption, leveling my gaze on some random guy I've never seen before.

"He's gonna dance with me," Joey says, pulling me toward her. "But don't go too far. You can have the next one." Joey smacks the guy's ass before sending him on his way.

"What the hell has gotten into you?" I pull her closer, attempting to hear her over the blaring music.

"Love sucks. I give my heart away too easily and the assholes I date continuously break it."

"You just haven't given it to the right asshole yet. Maybe he's closer than you think."

Joey's eyes light up, like a light bulb just went off in her head. "We need drinks." She runs toward the kitchen, disappearing into the crowd.

She pushes her way back through the crowd, then hops onto the coffee table, raising a shot glass into the air. "Can I have everyone's attention please?"

The music fades into quiet background noise and everyone turns to Joey.

"Thank you all for coming tonight to help me celebrate my birthday."

The group collectively cheers, raising their drinks into the air. "Earlier tonight, I found out my boyfriend has a wife and a baby on the way."

The group now boos in unison.

"No, no, no. It's okay, because their baby is going to be ugly! From now on, it's all about me. No more love, no more heartbreak. I believe the best way to get over someone is to get under someone else. Cheers to me getting laid on my birthday!"

The room roars with laughter, then someone kicks off a group rendition of "Happy Birthday".

Joey beams while they all sing to her, and when the song is over, I start toward her, but Ass Smack Guy beats me to helping Joey down from the coffee table. She turns to give me a thumbs up as she walks out to the patio with the next Mr. Wrong.

Once again, I've rescued Joey from her broken heart, just in time for the next guy to break it.

A gorgeous brunette with the most perfect tits money could buy confidently walks up to me, extending a beer in my direction.

I take it and nod my thanks.

"You've got some sexy dance moves there, handsome. Can I have the next dance?"

"You're cute, but you don't have to lie to kick it," I tease.

She flashes a wide grin. "Throwing in a little Ice Cube. Nice. I'm Breeann."

"Adam." I frown. "Ice Cube?"

"The rapper?" She tilts her head. "You Ain't Gotta Lie (Ta Kick It)" is one of his songs."

I shrug, not knowing the song.

"Looks like I have some things to teach you." She pulls me toward her, pressing her body against mine, so I wrap my arms around her waist and hold her close.

Our bodies begin a natural sway with the music, quickly moving closer together. With a little liquid courage in my system, dancing is much easier. My arms slide around her waist, pulling her fully against me.

"Did you come here alone?" I ask.

"I did, but I'm hoping not to leave the same way." Breeann lifts herself on her tiptoes bringing her lips to mine. Her kiss is soft, sweet, and tastes of the wine she's been drinking. When she pulls back, she licks her full bottom lip, then nods behind her. "There's too many people. Let's walk outside."

We link hands as she leads me to the patio.

When the sliding glass door opens, the moan hits my ears before the sight of Joey straddling the lap of Ass Smack Guy. His hands aggressively fondle everything under her shirt; her mouth is glued to his neck.

Well, that didn't take long. I close my eyes on a long blink.

"Damn, looks like that chick was serious about getting laid on her birthday."

"You don't know Johana?"

"Nope. My cousin lives down the street and we heard there was a party tonight. So, know of anywhere else?" she asks, raising an eyebrow in curiosity. "I'd much rather get to know you than talk about some drunk girl getting a titty hickey on the patio."

I look past her to Joey. With no regard for anyone around them, Ass Smack Guy has replaced his hand on her breast with his mouth.

My muscles tense. My empty hand curls into a fist at my side.

As the man who's been in love with Johana Warner since the seventh grade, to the desire to tear this slimeball limb from limb for being all over my girl burns hot in my veins.

As the guy who has been securely in the friendzone for the past sixteen years, I'm not going to say a damn thing.

Gritting my teeth against the ball of jealousy tightening in my gut, I give my head a quick shake and focus on the gorgeous brunette by my side. "Yeah. I know exactly where we can go." I grab Breeann's hand, we steal a few beers from the kitchen, then head upstairs.

For a brief moment, my goody-two-shoes angel appears on my shoulder telling me this is a mistake, but I flick the little fucker so hard he practically flies into next week.

Joey's bedroom door swings open with more force than I expected, slamming into the wall behind it. I kick it closed, knocking down the collection of purses Joey has hanging behind the door.

I crack the two beers open, hand Breeann one, then finishing mine in one long, cold swig.

"Whose room is this?" she asks, poking around items on the dresser.

"Johana's." Speaking her name aloud sends a fresh rush of pain through my chest.

But that's stupid. Johana isn't *mine.*

I don't care who she makes out with. No matter how many times she gets her heart broken, she'll never choose me to be the one to fix it.

Fuck, I wasn't even good enough to be her birthday break-up hook-up.

Never being much of a drinker, the multiple Jell-O shots and beers are starting to dull the chaotic thoughts in my head.

"I don't know what you're thinking about, but stop." Breeann puts her arms around my neck, pressing her body to mine. "You're really fucking hot," she whispers against my throat, her warm breath sending shockwaves straight to my dick.

"So are you." I slide my arms around her waist, taking a firm grip of her beautiful ass. Breeann jumps up and wraps her legs around my waist, causing me to lose my footing. We fall back onto Joey's bed with uncontrollable laughter.

I run my fingers through her thick brunette hair, tucking it gently behind her ear. She leans in, brushing her lips against mine. Needing something to push Joey out of my head, I cup Breeann's face and kiss her hard. My tongue strains to explore every inch of hers. My dick grows harder, uncomfortably pressing against the tight prison of my jeans.

"What the fuck are you doing?"

I freeze at the sound of Joey's voice.

"Whoops." Breeann giggles as we both look toward the patio door.

Joey and Ass Smack Guy stand just inside the room. Her eyes are wide and angry. "Who the hell are you? Get out of my room!"

"It's so okay," I slur, still trapped beneath Breeann. "She's with me."

"That makes it even worse," Joey snaps.

Breeann pushes off of me and rises to her feet, raising her hands. "My bad. Adam said you'd be cool with us getting to know each other in here."

"Well, he was wrong." She takes a step forward, eyes narrowed on Breeann.

"Hey." I stand up too quickly to run interference, and my drunk ass falls right into Ass Smack Guy's shirtless, six-pack abs.

"Come on, handsome, let's go. You can sleep this off with me at my cousin's place." Breeann helps me up, takes my hand, and we walk out of Joey's room without another word.

The sun burns my eyes like fire; my head pounds like a base drum at a rock concert. The three-block walk of shame is made worse by the fact that I forgot my keys, so I can't even just sneak away from Joey's place once I reach my car.

Maybe Isabella or Kenzie will open the door.

When I reach the condo, I look up at the door, shaking my head. My heart is heavy, and my memories of last night are fuzzy, but the angry look in Joey's eyes when she found me making out with Breeann on her bed is vivid and front-and-center in my mind.

Dragging my hand through my hair, I take a deep breath. It's now or never. Might as well get it over with. I take the stairs two at a time, and as I lift my hand to knock, the door swings open.

Joey's expressionless face gives nothing away. "Oh, look what the cat dragged in." She reaches for my set of keys, then holds them out for me.

"Figured you'd be back for these." She drops them into my palm and turns her back to settle onto the couch, focusing on her cup of coffee.

"Where's Ass Smack Guy?"

"You mean Brad?" she snaps.

"Oh, *of course* he's a Brad."

She lifts only her gaze. Her eyes are narrowed when they meet mine. "I sent him home last night. The mood was killed after I caught someone making out in my bed with a *child*."

"Breeann is twenty-two, and at least she didn't ditch her best friend to make out with some random dude on the patio."

Joey scoffs. "No, she chose to make out with *some random dude* on my *bed*."

Shaking my head, I run my hand over my neck. "She's a nice girl—"

"Well, why don't we top her with a cherry and call her your new best friend?" Joey rolls her eyes and dismisses me with the flick of her wrist. "Shouldn't you get back to *Breeann*?"

Clenching my teeth, I slam the front door on our conversation and head to my car.

Chapter Three

Adam

For our first official date, Bree asked to show me her wining and dining skills. I offered to take her anywhere she wanted to go but she insisted on cooking. We've been going out with friends for the past few weeks, but tonight is the first night we are staying in, just the two of us.

Pulling up to Bree's house, I grab the bottle of wine and flowers I brought her. I take a deep breath to calm my nerves. "Here goes nothing."

With the floor to ceiling windows, Bree sees me walk up and waves me in. "Hey, handsome." She greets me with a kiss, making me want much more than dinner.

"This house is amazing. I would have killed for a place like this at twenty-two. Truthfully, I'd kill for a place like this now." Floor to ceiling windows, hard wood floors, and some damn expensive entertainment system.

"My roommates and I do fairly well. Ready for dinner?"

"I think I'd rather start with dessert." I wrap my arms around her waist from behind, placing kisses along her exposed shoulders. Bree spins around, leaning against the counter, giving me full access to her beautiful chest.

"Maybe start with a little appetizer," she whispers. She slides her hand down between us and grabs a handful of my growing cock. "Just enough to get started." Bree winks, then lowers to her knees.

I begin to unbutton my pants, but my cell vibrates in my pocket.

"Either your phone is vibrating or you are way too excited to see me." She giggles.

"Sorry. I thought I shut this damn thing off." Pulling my phone from my pocket, my gaze lands on the screen. Joey has sent me three 911 texts. "Sorry. I have to take this."

I excuse myself to the front patio to call her back, my heart beating rapidly.

Joey picks up quickly. "Finally!"

"What's wrong? Are you okay?"

"No," she groans. "I'm on the worst date ever. This guy is just straight-up creepy. I need you to come rescue me."

"Seriously? That's why you text me with 911? To rescue you from a date?"

"Adam, please," Joey begs. "All this guy has talked about for a solid hour is the serial killer documentaries he's obsessed with."

"This better not be like last time, Joey. You could have taken that guy with one hand tied around your back. I'm on my first official date with Bree, and I would rather not leave if this is something you can handle. What about Bella? That girl can kick any man's ass."

"She's in New York for the week, visiting her parents."

I sigh, shaking my head. Resisting is futile; we both know I'm going to rescue her.

It's what I do.

"Please, Adam. I'm scared." Her voice cracks. She sounds genuine.

"Where are you?"

"I'll drop a pin."

"I'll be there as soon as I can." I end the call, then button the top button of my jeans. No killer blow job for me tonight.

"Everything good?" Bree asks as I walk back in the house.

"Not really. Johana's gotten herself into a scary situation and has asked me to help her out."

"Seriously? She doesn't have anyone else?" Bree slams the pan of lasagna onto the counter.

"She doesn't. Her father is the only man in her life, besides her half-brother."

"Why doesn't she call them?"

"One, they're not close. Two, he's touring in Europe somewhere right now. And three, she's my best friend." I kiss her on the forehead. "I'll call you after I get Joey home safely."

I may have just walked out on what could have been the best blowjob of my life, but I will never leave my best friend stranded and scared.

Chapter Four

Johana

Friday night, and there's no place I'd rather be. The beat of the music pulses through me. The heat of his body is pressed tightly against mine. Large hands grip my hips, pulling me back just enough to feel his erection graze my ass. I bend at the waist and grind against his dick.

"Oh, mamasita. You have no idea what you're doing to me right now," the stranger says in his sexy Spanish accent. He spins me around, pulling my body flush against his.

I gasp from the pressure against my core. "I know exactly what I'm doing because I know exactly what I want."

Eyes dark with lust, he leans down to bring his mouth to my ear. "Go tell your friends you're leaving with me."

"Am I now?"

Leaning down, he kisses a trail from my neck up to my ear and whispers, "I want to kiss every inch of your incredible body."

Goosebumps break out over my skin. "Yes *fucking* please." I grab his hand, dragging him to the table. Kenzie and Isabella look up at our approach with raised eyebrows.

"I'm leaving with…" *Shoot.* I forgot his name.

"Roberto," he says with the sexiest roll of his tongue.

Damn, I need this man to say some r-words on my clit.

"Jo." Kenzie stands, leveling me with her knowing gaze. "Are you sure?"

"I'm sure I'm about to have some hot sex with this hot man." I grab the bottle of Grey Goose from the bucket, take two huge swigs to polish it off, then place it upside down into the ice. Turning to Roberto, I smile. "Lead the way."

The unexpected humidity has every inch of fabric sticking to my body. I'm so ready to be naked with my new Latin Lover. A man this hot must have a house just as nice. A Laguna Beach mansion, overlooking the water, and a pool I plan to swim naked in.

The second the Uber driver hits the freeway and is no longer paying any attention to us, I unbuckle my seatbelt and straddle my way onto Roberto's lap. He fumbles with my buttons, exposing my bare breasts to him.

"Ma'am, I need you in your own seat, please. We'll be at your destination in just a couple minutes."

Roberto's arms tighten around my waist.

"Just a second," I gasp as Roberto's mouth closes over my nipple.

He sucks each nipple, giving each one playful flicks of the tongue. I bit my lip to contain the moan begging to escape. Roberto's strong hand slides up my thigh, disappearing beneath my black leather mini skirt, sliding my panties to the side. Two fingers glide right into my already wet and aching pussy.

"You are so tight. I can't wait to slide my cock in you," he whispers in my ear, causing my nipples to peak instantly.

The pad of his thumb circles my swollen clit. In complete ecstasy, I fling my head back, forgetting I'm in someone else's car, slamming into the driver's headrest.

"Ma'am." The car slows, then pulls to a stop. "In your seat, please."

Drunk and embarrassed, I slide off of Roberto and settle into my seat, avoiding the Uber driver's gaze in the rearview.

Roberto unclicks his seatbelt, then slides into the middle seat and buckles up again. "Happy?"

The Uber driver grunts a response, then pulls back out into traffic.

Roberto pulls me to him and I hide my face in his chest. "I can't wait to skinny dip in your pool," I whisper.

"I don't have a pool."

"A hot tub?" I ask.

He shakes his head. "But I have the next best thing, baby. Just you wait."

I open my eyes, blinded by the sun's penetrating glare, then quickly roll over, burying myself under the covers in an attempt to make the daylight and this jackhammer in my head disappear.

The bed moves, sending a wave of nausea through my stomach. What the fuck? Why does it feel like I'm on a raft? I was drunk last night, but not wake-up-the-next-morning-still-intoxicated drunk.

I move my body a bit, testing the waters. Yep. Water. My eyes widen. *Seriously? A waterbed?* No way. Who in their right mind has a freaking *waterbed* anymore? I peek my head out of the covers to see if I recognize where I am.

"Hola, mi amor."

Startled, I look up at the man standing in the doorway and a rush of disjointed memories flood my brain. "Umm. Hello?"

"Last night was magical." He plops down on the bed beside me, sending me on a wild wave ride, then runs his hand over my cheek reverently. "I want you to meet my mother."

My eyes widen. "Oh, I'm sorry. I need to get home to… um… feed my cat."

He frowns. "That's too bad. She's already cooking breakfast."

"Roberto!" a shrill voice screams from the kitchen. "How does your girlfriend like her eggs?"

Girlfriend? Holy crap, what have I gotten myself into?

Using the momentum from the waves, I jump from his bed, throw my dress on over my head, grab my shoes and purse, and sprint through the house and out the door as fast as my feet will carry me.

As I do the walk of shame out of some random apartment building, I shake my head. I have no idea where I am.

I fumble through my purse for my phone, then call Adam.

"Hello?"

"Hey, bestie."

"Good morning, Johana." His voice is groggy and tinged with annoyance. He breathes deeply, then sighs. "Let me guess, you need a ride?"

"Yes. I woke up in a freaking *waterbed.* Help me, please."

"Just call an Uber."

"I tried. I can't get one for over an hour."

"Fine. Where are you?"

"I have no idea. But it doesn't look safe. Just track my phone. Please hurry, Adam."

"You know you're a pain in my ass, right?"

"A thousand percent, but it's why you love me."

There's a Starbucks across the street, so I cross over and buy two coffees, then send Adam a picture. He'll hurry if there's caffeine waiting for him.

Close to thirty minutes later, Adam's black Jeep Wrangler finally pulls into the parking lot. I jump in before he even has time to turn the engine off.

"What in the hell did you get yourself into last night? Specially to end up on *this* side of town."

"I don't know. I went out with Kenzie and Isabella and got completely wasted. I went home to Roberto's mother's house and spent the night on his nineteen-eighties waterbed." I say it cheerfully like it totally makes sense and there's absolutely nothing weird about Roberto and his mother and his waterbed.

"You know your friends are kind of shitty, right? They should have never let you go home with some random guy."

"Okay, Mother Teresa. Like you've never had a one-night stand."

"Once, in college. You know that's not my thing."

"Seriously? Not even a few wild jumps in the sack after a breakup?"

"Why is it so hard for you to believe I'm not like you?" Adam's tone is sharp.

"That was way harsh." I turn my body and stare out the window; I don't want him seeing the tears burning my eyes.

"Joey, I'm sorry. I know your break-up with Ian was hard, but I don't think these one-night stands are helping."

"They might be." I pout like a child being scolded.

"Alright." He sighs as he guides the Jeep onto the freeway. After a moment, he says, "Well, do you feel better?"

"That's not the point."

"What if one of these guys hurts you?"

"I'm twenty-eight, Adam. I think I can take care of myself."

"Can you? Then why is this the third time I've picked you up in the last month?"

"Because you always pick up the pieces when my life is a mess." I curl up into a ball, protecting myself from Adam's knowing gaze.

"Everyone, I'd like you to meet Johana Warner. Her family just relocated here from San Francisco. Let's make her feel welcome."

The groans fill the classroom. I've become numb to them; I've been to three schools in the last five years. This is my first new middle school, so it's a little scarier.

"There's a seat over there next to Adam," the teacher says. "Adam, raise your hand so our new friend knows where to sit."

The girls in the class simultaneously giggle.

Great. Of course, the teacher would have to put me next to the dorky kid. Braces, big glasses, the whole nine yards.

"Hi," I say nervously as I take the seat next to him.

"Hey, Joey. Welcome to Newport Beach."

I'm taken aback when he calls me Joey. No one besides my mother uses that nickname. Instinct makes me want to correct him and tell him my name is Johana, yet, for the first time in a long while, allowing him to call me Joey feels safe.

"Let me see your schedule and I'll see if we have any classes together."

I dig the piece of paper out of the back pocket of my jeans and hand it to him.

"We have the next three classes together. I can show you around."

"Cool." Yay me.

When the two-thirty bell rings, I quickly escape the double doors of Newport Shores Middle School to wait for my ride home. The first half of the day was spent with Adam talking my ear off and after lunch not a single person talked to me.

"Hey, Joey! How was your first day?" Adam shouts from behind me.

"Okay, I guess."

"Cool. See you tomorrow." He takes off down the hill the same time my half-siblings' nanny pulls up.

"Hurry up, Johana. I need to get you home before I go pick up Luna and Lincoln."

"Sorry."

When my dad and stepmother told me they were getting a nanny for the twins, I wished for Mrs. Doubtfire, but instead, we got Ingrid—the wicked witch of the west.

Ingrid stops just long enough for me to jump out of the minivan. Getting home to decorate my new room has been the only bright light to this miserable day. My room is my piece of heaven. I'm not even five feet up the driveway when my stepmother's shrill voice pierces my eardrums.

"This is my house. Nothing from Charlotte needs to be here."

Excuse me. Did I just hear her right? I creep up to the side of the house to get a better view of them and make sure I'm hearing things correctly.

"Crystal, don't be ridiculous. Everyone knows this is your house, but Charlotte is Johana's mother. I can't just erase her from our home."

"She died four years ago. Johana needs to move on. Plus, it's too late. I already donated all the boxes to charity."

"You did what?" I scream.

My step-monster turns toward me, a smug smile on her too-big lips. "The box with all your snow globes, dolls, and silly little things. Gone. I left it on the curb and it was picked up an hour ago."

"I hate you!" I run past them, throw my backpack down in the entryway, then continue through the backdoor and onto the beach, running until my feet hit the water.

"Why!" I scream, finally letting my tears fall.

A random golden retriever appears beside me, nudging my leg with a ball in its mouth.

"Where did you come from?" I ask, like the dog is supposed to answer me.

"Snuffy! Snuffy!" A young child runs along the shoreline, calling out for her lost puppy.

Rubbing the dog's ears, I smile through my tears. "I have a feeling you might be Snuffy. Come on, let's get you home."

I turn around, my eyes widening as Adam and a young girl approach me. "I think he might belong to you," I say.

"Snuffbubbles, you can't run away anymore." The girl hugs her dog tight.

"You live around here?" Adam asks.

"Yeah, we just moved into the white one over there."

"Cool. We're the blue one next door."

Seriously, what are the odds?

"Everything okay? I heard some yelling over there earlier."

"No. My stepmother is awful and I hate her. She threw away a box of my stuff she had no right to touch."

"Was it important?"

"It was all the things my mother gave me before she died."

His eyes widen. "And she just threw it away?"

"She said she donated it to charity."

"Oh geez. That sucks."

My cell phone buzzes in my pocket.

Dad: Please come home so we can talk about this.

I'm not ready to talk. I'm just as mad at him as I am at her because he let this happen.

"Do you have to go?" Adam asks.

"No." I shove the phone back into my pocket without responding.

"Let me take Mandi home and we can go get some ice cream."

"I'd like that."

The entire drive is silent.

I *know* my life's a mess. Ian fucked me up, and if one-nighters with random guys is helping me get over him, so be it. And if Adam doesn't agree with me, maybe we don't need to be friends anymore. The thought sends a rush of pain through my chest.

Adam pulls the car to a stop in front of my condo. "Want me to come up?"

"No, I'm good. I'll Venmo you some gas money."

"Johana, stop. I didn't mean to upset you."

"Well, you did." I climb out quickly and slam the door so he can't respond, then I hurry up the stairs and slip inside.

"Kenzie! Isabella! Where are you?" I scream for my roommates as I charge up the stairs.

"On the patio," Kenzie calls. "Get your suit on. It's beautiful out here."

I make my way to the back deck, scowling as I look between them.

"Jo, what happened? What's wrong?" Isabella stands, searching my face.

"How could you guys just let me go home with some random guy when I was so drunk?"

Kenzie raises her hands in defense. "Don't blame us. I asked you if you were sure. Once you polished off the rest of the vodka, I knew there was no arguing with you. I know how *Drunk Jo* gets."

"Plus, I turned the tracker on your phone so I knew where you were the whole time." Isabella waves her phone in the air.

I huff. That's good, I guess. At least they could have tracked my corpse down if they needed to.

"So?" Kenzie asks, dragging out the *o*. "How was it?"

"Awkward, from what I can remember. Which isn't much. I woke up in a waterbed."

"No way." Isabella is struggling to contain her laughter.

"Oh," I say, "go ahead and let it out, because it gets better. He lives with his *mother*, who was cooking us breakfast when I woke up."

My friends can no longer contain their laughter.

"Oh my god," Isabella says, "please tell us you stayed."

"Absolutely not. I threw on my dress and did a walk of shame until Adam came to get me."

Kenzie snorts. "That must have gone over well."

"Yeah, well, Mr. High and Mighty can go fuck himself. Judging me because I enjoy one-night stands?" I dismiss Adam with a flick of my wrist.

"Girl, forget about Adam. Forget about the guy from last night. Forget about *boys*, period. Go get your bathing suit on and enjoy this day with us."

"I have something to cheer you up." Isabella waggles her eyebrows as I return with a fresh bottle of prosecco. "I scored us invites to Bennett Blakely's thirty-third birthday next weekend. It's a private event at his Malibu beach house."

My mouth drops open. No fucking way. "*The* Bennett Blakely? From *Hope's Landing*? How did you pull this one off?"

"My brother tattoos his brother. He told him to come and bring some hot chicks."

"And her brother thought of us." Kenzie splays her hands out. "Naturally."

"Who else does a gay tattoo artist bring to a straight guy's party besides his sister and her smoking-hot friends?" Isabella adds.

"Hopefully, next weekend I'll wake up in a Malibu mansion rather than an outdated waterbed in some guy's mother's house."

"Or you could just make it home to wake up in your own bed," Kenzie suggests.

"Where's the fun in that?" Isabella teases.

Chapter Five

Adam

One of these days, Joey is just going to push me too far and I won't come running to her rescue. She'll call, and I won't answer.

Ugh. Who am I kidding?

There will never be a day I won't answer the phone for Johana Warner.

I knew the day Joey walked into my seventh-grade homeroom class she would be special to me.

"Where was she this time?" Breeann asks, still lying in bed, waiting for me to return.

"Somewhere out past Disneyland. We got into a fight. I told her she shouldn't be doing this stuff because she's gonna get hurt."

Bree snorts. "I bet she took that well." She rolls over, propping up on one elbow to look at me. "Adam, you need to stop being her personal driver. If she wakes up in some guy's bed, let her figure out how she's going to get home. Johana's a big girl."

"Which is what she said right before she slammed the car door on our conversation."

"Maybe it's time you took a break from your friendship with Johana and focused more on what's right in front of you." She pulls the sheets down, exposing her perfectly sculpted naked body. "I have a lot to offer, if you just give me a chance."

"Yeah?" I scoot my body closer to hers, running my hand down her side and over her hip to grip her ass.

Bree leans forward and crushes her lips to mine, taking full control of my mouth. Even first thing in the morning, her mouth tastes like sweet strawberries.

I slide my arm under her, pulling her body on top of mine. "Tell me, babe, what is it you would like?"

"I want to be your girlfriend, not just the girl you have a good time with on Friday night."

"If it makes you feel better, you're the only person I'm having a good time with on Friday nights." Wrapping my arms around her, I nuzzle her nose with mine. "Bree, you know I don't do relationships. They've never been my thing. And my work schedule doesn't allow me much free time."

"Is this about Johana?"

"I've told you before, Joey is my best friend. Nothing more." The words tighten a fist around my heart, but I push the feeling aside.

Bree's eyes narrow, searching my gaze, then she says, "Am I really the only girl you're having a good time with?"

"Yes."

"So, are we exclusive?"

I'm not really into relationships, but Bree is as close as I've gotten to one for a long time, so… "Sure." I pat her bottom with both hands. "Go get dressed and we'll grab some food before my shift."

Bree squeals, then leans down to kiss me again before bouncing off the bed.

I lay there, listening to Bree in the shower and trying not to focus on the way my heart ached when I said Joey and I are nothing but friends.

Since Joey moved here, we've become best friends. We didn't hang out much at school because she made new friends, but over the summer, when all those friends were gone, she and I became the dynamic duo. And now, I've finally worked up the nerve to tell her how I feel. I want to start my eighth-grade year with my first girlfriend.

I've got the perfect plan. I'm going to wait until we're stopped at the top of the Ferris Wheel, and then I'll ask her to be my girlfriend. It works all the time in those romantic movies my mom likes to watch.

We've been at the Fun Zone for an hour now, and its finally time. As we wait in line for our turn on the Ferris wheel, someone calls Johana's name.

Both of us turn, searching the crowd.

Royce rushes toward us, her entourage of friends on her heels.

"Oh my god!" Joey screeches, bouncing on her toes. "Royce! You're back!"

The girls slam so hard into each other they almost topple to the ground.

When Royce pulls back, she shoots me a glare, then focuses on Joey. "Daddy's yacht broke down and we had to use the helicopter to get home. It was so tragic. Come on, I'm meeting Zuri at the arcade."

"I'll be over there in a minute. I'm going to ride the Ferris Wheel with Adam."

Royce's icy glare flicks to me, then back to Joey. "Are you guys, like, a thing now?" Her words drip with disgust.

"Me? With Adam? No. He's just my neighbor."

Joey's words punch me in the gut. Just her neighbor?

"Have fun." Royce giggles. "Meet us when you're done."

"You can go with your friends," I say.

"You're my friend, too, Adam."

"Am I? Or am I just your neighbor?"

Joey frowns. "Adam, you know we're friends."

"I'm just not cool enough to be your friend in front of Royce?"

"Stop. You are plenty cool. Let's ride the Ferris Wheel and go hang out with the girls."

"We'll ride the Ferris wheel, then you can go catch up with your friends rather than hang out with your geeky neighbor."

"You're a pretty amazing guy, Adam." Joey leans over, surprising me with a kiss on the cheek. "We're going to find you a girlfriend this year."

Bree exits the bathroom, all smiles and energy to spare. Her eyes dance with happiness, such a stark contrast to the way my heart sits heavy in my chest.

"Ready!" Bree pops me out of my self-pity party. What she said earlier was spot-on. I need to focus on what's right in front of me. I need to stop wallowing in my past and start living for my future. Breeann and I might have something here. I mean, she's smart, driven, and drop dead gorgeous. I should at least give us a fair shot.

I follow her out the door and down the stairs, watching every perfect curve bounce with each step. Her long, straight, brown hair blows across her shoulders in the warm ocean breeze. Turning around to see if I'm following her, Breeann smiles, sending sparks directly to my heart.

And my dick.

She slows down and waits for me to catch up, then links her fingers with mine as we walk across the street to the neighborhood café. "What do you think Johana is going to say?" she asks.

"About?"

"Us officially dating, silly. You know she doesn't like me."

The hostess greets us with a warm smile, then leads us to a quiet booth toward the back of the restaurant. I settle in across from Bree and open my menu. "You two just met under bad circumstances. The night we met, Johana had *just* found out her boyfriend was a married man about to have a child. She wasn't in the best place."

Breeann snorts. "She wasn't very happy to catch us making out in her bed."

I lean across the table and give her a peck on the nose. "But it was so much fun."

"Maybe we could have her over for dinner soon."

I grimace, but Bree is focused on her open menu. "Let's not push it." Joey is one stubborn woman.

Chapter Six

Adam

"Adam?" Carol calls. "Are you here?"

Fuck. Things have finally calmed down enough for me to take a five-minute break and close my eyes, and now the head nurse is looking for me.

"Yeah," I grumble. As much as I want to ignore her, I can't.

Tonight has been hell in the ER. A drunk driver hit a car full of teenagers. Luckily, everyone is going to be okay, but it was a fight.

"You were fantastic tonight," Carol says.

"Just doing my job."

"Not everyone can talk to parents the way you do. No matter the situation, you're able to stay calm." She grins proudly. "Just like your father."

"I learned from the best."

"Go home," she says. "The kids are stable, and we've got it covered. You've had a rough couple of days."

"You don't have to tell me twice. Thanks, Carol."

Driving home, I replay tonight's events in my head; from driving up to the horrific scene, assisting in surgery and finally being able to tell the young girl's parents their daughters were going to be fine. As hard as tonight was, it's the reason I became an ER nurse. I love saving lives.

Even though I'm exhausted, my adrenaline is still ramped up and I'm just not ready to call it a night. I hit the Bluetooth button on my steering wheel.

"Call Joey."

She picks up after two rings. "You know I'm still mad at you, right?"

"Yes, Joey, I know you're still mad. It's not the first time and I'm sure it won't be the last. But it doesn't matter. Tradition is tradition. I'll pick you up in fifteen minutes for ice cream."

"It's ten o'clock at night. Nothing is open anymore and I'm already in my pajamas. Let's just do it tomorrow."

"We'll get ice cream from the 7-11 and eat in my car."

"Now, how can I resist such an offer? See you in a minute," she says with a chuckle.

When I pull up to her condo, she's already waiting out front.

I smile as she climbs into the Jeep. "I knew you couldn't stay mad at me."

"Not when you offer me ice cream. Rough night?"

"Yeah, a drunk driving accident." I wait for her to buckle up, then pull back out onto the road. "Older man ran a red light and hit a group of teenage kids. The young girl I was assisting was banged up pretty bad. She had some broken ribs and a ruptured spleen. But we got her into surgery quickly enough to save her life."

"And still celebrating with ice cream." Joey flashes me a grin.

When Joey and I were fifteen, we witnessed a car hit a guy on a skateboard on our way to the fun zone, and we were the first to call 911. The officer told us that because of our quick actions, a man's life was saved.

It was at that moment that I knew I wanted to help people. And it was the first time that Joey and I celebrated saving lives with ice cream. It's been our tradition ever since.

"I'm sorry for what I said the other morning." I hold the door for her to step into the convenience store. She beelines for the ice cream freezer in the back corner.

Following, I stop behind her and look at the selections over her shoulder. "The things I said were harsh and definitely not okay. I just worry about you, Joey. You're my best friend."

"It's okay." She reaches into the freezer and grabs our two favorites, then turns toward me and holds them up.

I nod, and Joey flashes a grin.

As we wait in line to check out, her grin slowly falls. "I know I haven't been the easiest person to be around since my break-up with Ian." She sighs. "Getting plastered at clubs and going home with random guys probably isn't what I should be doing."

"But, if it's what you want to do, I have no right to judge you."

"*Yes*, you do. It's what friends do. I mean, I judge you on your taste in women all the time." She laughs as she takes my twenty and hands it to the cashier. "Which, by the way, is still horrible."

"Speaking of my taste in women—"

Joey groans. "Please tell me you got rid of Breeann."

I accept my change and lead Joey back outside to the car. "Actually, just the opposite. I think she may be my girlfriend."

Joey stops dead in her tracks by the hood of the car. "Ugh! What am I going to do with you?"

I nudge her with my shoulder, then go open the passenger door and wait for her to start moving again. When she stands there, I raise my eyebrows.

Finally, she steps around me and climbs into the car, shaking her head.

She'll get over me and Breeann, just like I get over every guy she dates.

Instead of me.

Chapter Seven

Johana

I've been watching Bennett Blakely on *Hope's Landing* for as long as I can remember. The nanny my father hired after my mother died was obsessed with the show. She would have it on every afternoon while I did my homework. It wasn't long before I was skipping homework to watch with her.

Tonight, I'm going to Bennett's thirty-third birthday party. I keep pinching myself to make sure it's not a dream.

The biggest challenge is figuring out what to wear. I want to look hot but not slutty, available but not desperate, willing but not eager. You never know who will be at this party.

For a solid fifteen minutes, I tear every piece of clothing out of my closet. "I'm not going," I scream to my roommates.

"Excuse me? Like hell you're not." Isabella storms into my room. I love her no-bullshit sass. It's one of the things that drew me to be her friend. Bella is thin and tall, with legs for days; her jet-black hair is cut short, tightly framing her face.

"What's going on? If Jo's not going, I'm not going." Kenzie is the shy introvert of our trio; she'd rather stay home than go out partying.

"We're going. This is *Bennett Blakely's* party. It's not like this is an everyday invitation. It's Bennett Blakely. Mr. Ryan Hope in the flesh. I mean seriously, Jo, haven't you been crushing on this guy since high school? He's single. You're single."

I bark out a laugh. "Seriously? Bennett Blakely would never date someone like me."

"Why not?" Isabella asks.

I wait for her to laugh, but she watches me expectantly. Oh. She's serious. "For starters, I'm not famous. He's known for only dating celebrities. And second, I'm not his type." I grab my phone off my bed and search Bennett's girlfriends. "See. All teeny, little things with not a single curve on their body. Do you see this booty?" I bend and wiggle my ass at Isabella.

She rolls her eyes, then smacks at me. "You have a great ass. Now squeeze it into that slinky little number you bought on Rodeo Drive a few months back. The dress is a stunner."

"I seriously can't believe we're on our way to a party at Bennett Blakely's house," Kenzie says from the squished middle back seat of the Uber.

"And you're sure we're on the guest list?" I ask. "It would suck to get all the way there just to find out your brother is an idiot."

"Even if he didn't put us on the list, one look at you in that dress and we'll be on *everyone's* guest list," Isabella retorts.

I'm well blessed in the area of tits and ass, but I've never used them as a way to pick up men. Isabella, on the other hand, likes to use them as her go-to weapon.

"Did you tell Adam where you were going tonight?" Kenzie asks.

"No. He's not my babysitter. Plus, he has a girlfriend now to worry about."

"Who?" they ask in unison.

"Remember the chick he was making out with in my bed at my birthday party?"

They both gasp.

"That's her. Breeann."

"You say her name like it upsets you," Isabella says with an accusatory eyebrow wiggle.

"Um, no. Adam can just do a lot better than some twenty-two-year-old *child*."

"Sounds like someone's a bit jealous," she continues to press.

"Uh, no. Bite your tongue."

Isabella laughs. "Eat a bag of dicks."

"I intend to."

"Ugh, the two of you are nasty." Kenzie shudders dramatically.

"Which is why you love us."

"Holy shit." The words slip out of my mouth before I can hold them back. There are more people crammed into this room than at some concerts I've been to. The beat from the music is already causing my eardrums to vibrate.

"C'mon, let's go grab a drink." Isabella grabs my hand, pushing her way through the crowd. I grab on to Kenzie's, so we don't lose her.

To my left, male and female strippers dance on a stage. To my right, a man with tigers sits surrounded by more hot girls in bikinis.

I'm not sure what I expected a Bennett Blakely party to be like, but this definitely isn't it.

"This is crazy," Kenzie says with a worried look in her eyes.

"I know! Isn't it great?" Isabella hands us each a glass of champagne. "Let's go dance."

Downing our drinks, we push our way to the middle of the dance floor. Big crowd or not, Bella is always the center of attention. Kenzie and I are just along for the ride.

It doesn't take long for a group of hot young guys to join us with another round of drinks. Despite being obviously too young, I'm not going to turn down free drinks and a sexy grinding partner. The more drinks he brings, the harder I grind.

"When are you going to strip?" the stranger whispers in my ear.

"Excuse me?"

"Your body is so fucking hot. I want to see you strip."

"What the fuck!" I slap his face with such force his head spins.

Where the fuck are Bella and Kenzie when I need them? Great. I'm alone, my hand stings like a bitch, and now I have to pee.

Lost and pushing my way through the crowd of people, I make my way upstairs in search of a bathroom without a line of fifty people. The first two doors I try are locked. The third swings wide open.

Standing there in just a pair of board shorts, is *the* Bennett Blakely. Six feet of a perfectly sculpted, tan god stands in front of me. My mouth opens, but not a single sound comes out.

"Can I help you?" he asks in his deep voice with the slight southern drawl, causing my body to cover in goosebumps.

"Oh my god. I'm so sorry. I was just looking for a bathroom. I'll… I'll go wait in the line downstairs."

"Don't be silly. A gorgeous woman like you should never have to wait in line. Please, use mine."

My cheeks heat, and electricity buzzes through my veins under the weight of his stare, but I manage to step inside without stumbling or giggling or gushing about how much I love him, or how I've been watching him for years and I'm his biggest fan.

He smiles as I approach him, then motions toward his en suite bathroom. "Right this way."

"Thank you." My words sound okay, no hint of *obsessed fan* in my voice. Phew.

Bennett places his hand on the small of my back and all the cells in my body rush to meet his palm. He leads me further into the suite, then motions toward the bathroom. "Take your time."

I make my way to the bathroom and slip inside, then close the door and resist the urge to jump up and down. With these heels, he'd hear me for sure. Instead, I scream silently, digging my phone out of my purse to text the girls because holy shit, I'm in Bennett *freaking* Blakely's bedroom right now.

I will never recover.

I sit down on the toilet, and…

Freeze.

Nothing will come out.

Stage fright robs me of basic bodily functions. What if Bennett hears me *pee*?

What if I accidently *fart*?

Oh god.

I don't think I could ever leave this bathroom if that happened. Maybe I can just wait him out. He should be heading back down to the party any minute, right? Yeah. Then I can go.

"Everything okay in there?" he shouts from the bedroom.

Fuck. How long have I been here?

"Yeah," I sheepishly answer. I close my eyes and think about anything else besides whose toilet I'm sitting on. Finally, my body spurs into action and remembers what it's naturally made to do. When I'm finished, I wash my hands and do my best to quickly smooth any fly-always, then grin at the mirror to check my teeth. I apply a quick coat of gloss, blow myself a kiss in the mirror, then head out.

"Sorry to keep you from your party, Mr. Blakely," I say as I enter his bedroom.

"No worries. I'm not headed down there anyways." He leans his butt against his pool table and crosses his tan, toned arms over his chest, then drags his gaze down my body appreciatively.

I pull in a ragged breath as subtly as I can, even though heat spreads out over my skin as if not just his eyes grazed me, but his hands. "But... isn't this your birthday party?"

"My birthday is my cousin's excuse to throw a raging party at my house. I guess at twenty-three, partying with strippers was all I wanted. I gotta cut the kid some slack."

"And now?" Shit. Those words came out without me even thinking about them.

"Now? Now, I'd like the company of a beautiful young woman to walk along the beach with me."

"Well, I hope you find someone." I turn to leave.

"Seriously? I know I'm not so good at this, but it was obvious."

"Huh?"

"I let you use my toilet. The least you could do is indulge me in a walk, Miss...?"

"Johana. Johana Warner," I stammer.

"Well, Miss Johana Warner, would you like to blow this crazy stripper party and go talk a walk along the beach with me?"

"Me? Really?"

"Unless there's another Johana around here, but you're the only gorgeous woman I see."

Bennett gently takes my hand, leading me down the staircase and out the back door through the maze of people. He grabs two glasses of champagne and nods his head for me to follow.

"So, strippers and tigers aren't your thing?" I ask, trying to break the ice.

His eyes widen almost comically. "There are *tigers*? Tigers in my *home*?"

"Yup. Petting baby tiger cubs is apparently the newest fad. You didn't know your cousin was planning all this?"

"Not a thing. I asked him to housesit for a few weeks while I was in Canada shooting a holiday movie. I came home tonight to all this chaos. Todd's still a kid who needs to grow up." He tilts his head. The unmistakable desire in his eyes is a tether to my core, which tightens into a knot of want the longer he holds my gaze. "How did you end up here? You don't seem like one of my cousin's groupies."

"I'm not sure if I should take that as an insult or a compliment." I tilt my head in confusion.

"Definitely a compliment." He runs his tongue over his bottom lip. "You seem way too classy to be hanging out with the likes of Todd."

"My roommate's brother tattoos your cousin and told him to bring some hot chicks with him to the party. Being a gay man in Hollywood, my roommates and I are the only chicks he knows."

Bennett raises his glass. "Cheers to brothers and random bathroom searches." We clink our glasses together and laugh. We continue to walk along the shore as we sip our drink. "So, roommates, huh? Boyfriend roommate?"

"No. No boyfriend. I live with two of my sorority sisters from college, Isabella and Kenzie. My father bought me a condo for graduation. I hate being alone, so now we all live together."

"Where did you go to college?"

"Stanford."

"What was your major?"

"Journalism."

"What do you do now?"

"I'm a freelance writer. You ask a lot of questions, Mr. Blakely." I flirtatiously bump my shoulder into him.

"It's because I want to know everything I can about you, Miss Warner." He leans down, placing a soft kiss on my cheek. He gently drags his lips to my ears and whispers, "If you'll let me."

My knees attempt to give out from under me. My skin ripples with goosebumps. My nipples peak from excitement. Did Bennett Blakely just say he wants to get to know me? Maybe I'm actually passed out drunk in a corner and this is just an amazing dream.

"I think we can figure something out." Despite the cool ocean breeze, every inch of my body is flush with heat.

Bennett's lips melt into mine with the gentlest of kisses. As if testing the waters, his tongue slowly caresses mine. Moaning into his mouth, our kiss deepens. Within seconds, the butterflies are swirling through my entire body.

"Damn. Better than Mama's sweet tea," he whispers, as we break for a breath. Just as he leans in for the second kiss, sirens scream in the distance.

Bennett's phone rings.

"Those sirens better not be heading to my house, Todd," he says when he answers the call. I hear his brother screaming on the other end but I can't make out what he says. "You've got to be fucking kidding me." He ends the call and pins me with those gorgeous eyes. "C'mon, sweet lips. I gotta get back to the house. There's been an accident."

Bennett links his fingers in mine, and we race back to the house.

Chapter Eight

Adam

"Move back! I need everybody out!" Even over the crowds of people I can hear the young woman screaming from the other room.

"Alright, I've got you now." I approach the young woman and begin assessing her injuries. Her leg has a deep bite wound but nothing we can't fix up with some stitches. "Can someone tell me what happened?"

"These are my cubs. I was hired to bring them as entertainment. One got spooked when a drunk stripper tripped over him and the cub bit this young lady."

"Whose party is this?"

"Mine." A young man steps up.

Damn kid, throwing a party at his parents' beach mansion.

"But it's my house. I'm Bennett Blakely. I'll cooperate in any way necessary."

Looking up at the voice I've heard many times before, I'm taken aback to see Joey standing right behind him.

My eyes lock on her, but she can't stop staring at the victim. Joey looks like she's about to pass out; she's never been one for blood. Before I can say anything, Isabella and Kenzie grab her arm and pull her outside with them.

"The police are going to want to talk to you, Mr. Blakely," I say.

"Of course, no problem. Please excuse me." He races out the same door the girls just left through. Was Joey here with Bennett Blakely tonight? Surely, if my best friend had a date with her high school celebrity crush, she'd tell me, right?

"You guys got this?" I check with my partners before taking off after the girls.

I freeze when I see Bennett Blakely's arm around my Joey. I guess she is here with him. Maybe we're not as good of friends as I thought we still were.

"Hey, ladies," I say, approaching my group of friends. "I'm glad to see you're all okay."

"Oh, hey, Adam. What are you doing here?" Isabella asks, a hint of annoyance in her tone.

"One of the EMTs got sick, so I'm filling in. Joey, can I talk to you for a minute?" I ask, directing my attention to her.

"Actually, my driver is here to take the ladies home." Bennett boldly steps in and interrupts us. "If you need a statement from Miss Warner, you can go through my lawyer.".

"Bennett, it's okay." Joey brushes his arm and the hairs on the back of my neck stand straight up. "This is Adam, my childhood best friend."

"Oh, sorry, man. It's great you two still keep in touch. Hopefully, you can catch up again soon, but right now I'd like to get my girl out of here."

His *girl*? What the actual fuck?

As much as I want to go chasing after Joey, I'm still on duty and I need to get back to my victim. Fortunately for me, I know the officer taking Bennett's statement; I'll hit him up later for the details.

On the way back to the hospital, I send Joey a text.

Me: *What a coincidence we were at the same party tonight. Glad you're safe and Bennett Blakely took care of "his girl".*

Joey's broken my heart *again*. When will I stop allowing it? When will I stop thinking I'll ever be anything more than the guy who's always available to save her from her bad decisions?

Why did I even come? Parties are not my thing. I don't have any friends here and I wasn't even invited. Yet, somehow, Joey still convinced me to go. She tells me I need to get out more and make more friends. I tell her I've got plenty of friends, but she insists internet chat room people are not real friends.

The real reason Joey asks me along is because her dad will only let her go if I'm with her. We leave together and then I usually don't see her again until it's time to go home. My friends tell me all the time that Joey is just using me, but I see it as something friends do for each other.

Being the skinny computer guy in a high school full of elite jocks, I feel like an outcast. Joey has tried giving me a makeover, but there's no making a mountain out of this mole hill. I like who I am; I just wish the girls did. I wish Joey did.

As the night progresses, the drinking starts. I feel like a creep sitting here, just watching Joey, waiting for her to tell me when we're going home. Maybe the guys are right. Maybe, I am a fucking pussy. What else do you call a guy who takes the girl he's in love with to a party to watch her make out with some other guy?

The sirens break my chain of thought. Fuck. The cops.

In a mad fury, people are running everywhere. I lose sight of Joey. I make my way to the top of the hill, where she'll have to pass me to get off the beach and I can get her home.

"Johana!" I scream as she starts up the hill. She doesn't hear me. "Johana!"

Jimmy Berkin has got her by the wrist and is practically dragging her up the hill. Shit. Joey's wasted.

"Joey, come on. Let's go home so you don't get in trouble with your dad." I try to jump between her and Jimmy.

"I've got my girl, pipsqueak." Without even an effort, he pushes me, sending me tumbling backward down the hill.

When I make it back up the hill, the parking lot is empty. With a badly twisted ankle, I hobble home.

During my fifteen-minute walk, I can't decide what hurts worse: my ankle, my pride, or my heart. What I do know is I hate the way Johana Warner makes me feel.

"How the hell could you be so irresponsible? What kind of example are you setting for your siblings?" Joey's dad is yelling at her in the front yard. I attempt to pass by unnoticed.

"And you!" he yells.

Fuck, he saw me.

"I asked you to keep an eye on her."

"Sorry, Mr. Warner." Do I lie and cover for Joey again? Or do I let her get in trouble finally? "After I fell and got hurt, Jimmy said he'd bring Johana home for me."

I'm an idiot.

"Then why is she drunk and you're not?"

"You know what, Mr. Warner? Why don't you ask Jimmy Berkin? As much as I want to spend time with Joey, she'd rather be with him." Without giving either of them the chance to say anything more, I take off toward my house.

When I slam the door behind me, my father knows something happened.

"Wanna talk about it?" he asks.

"No." I shake my head. "Question?"

"Shoot."

"Is the offer to spend the summer in Hawaii with Uncle Nick still available?"

"Of course."

"Can I leave tomorrow?" I ask.

"Son, what happened tonight?"

"Nothing. I just decided I don't want to spend the summer in Newport Beach and I want to leave ASAP."

"All right, I'll see what I can do."

"Thanks, Dad."

Twenty-four hours later, I'm sitting on the tarmac at LAX, waiting for my plane to Kauai to leave. I haven't returned any of Joey's calls or texts all day. It's just a never-ending circle with her. She apologizes, I forgive her, and the same thing happens again next time we go out. Honestly, I'm done with it.

My thoughts are interrupted by the vibrations in my pocket. I pull out my phone to see who's texted me.

Joey: *What's going on? I just went to your house and Mandi said you left for the summer. I hope this isn't true.*

Fuck it. I need to tell her.

Me: *Yup. Going to spend some time with my Uncle Nick.*

Joey: *Why? Is this because of last night? I thought we were going to learn how to drive together.*

Me: *I'm sure Jimmy can teach you.*

Joey: *I'll miss you.*

The pounding on my door is loud enough to wake the neighbors in the entire condo complex.

"I'm coming! I'm coming!" I stumble my way to the front door, opening it without checking the peephole to see who's here.

"Seriously?" Joey snaps. "Can't you ever just be happy for me? Why do you always have to be such a dick?" She stands too close to the door, like she might have been trying to look into the peephole from the wrong side. Her jaw is set angrily and her eyes are bright with indignation.

"Well, good morning to you, too, sunshine."

Joey scoffs.

I drag my hand through my hair. "And what are you talking about?"

"Your snotty little text last night, after running into me at the party?"

I raise an eyebrow. "Were you planning on telling me, your *random* childhood best friend, that you are now Bennett Blakely's girl?"

Joey crosses her arms over her chest. "I just met him last night. Bella's brother invited us. I accidently walked into Bennett's bedroom, and then we went on a walk."

"And, poof, you became his girl?" I question.

"We have a spark."

Damn, there's the twinkle Joey gets in her eyes when she's crushing on someone. She steps inside, brushing past me to make herself at home on my couch.

My heart breaks for this girl. Again. With a deep breath of resignation—because she really will never be mine—I close the door and turn toward her. "Just be careful. I've read he's a Hollywood playboy."

"You've *read* he's a playboy?" she asks, raising an eyebrow in utter confusion.

"Breeann's bathroom is filled with those gossip magazines. They're entertaining as hell when you forget your phone while taking a shit."

"Ew. TMI." She tosses a pillow at me. "Hurry up, we have to be at brunch in thirty minutes."

"I asked Bree to meet us there."

"Ugh. Why go and ruin a good Sunday Funday?"

"Because I'm dating her and I want her there. So, let me get this straight? It's okay for you not to like my girlfriends, but I'm supposed to like all the guys you date?"

She grins. "Duh. Now you're getting it."

Her giggle has always made me smile. Shaking my head, I concede. "If you learn to play nice with Breeann, I'll give Bennett a chance."

"I'm not making any promises." She crosses her arms over her chest and juts out her chin.

Oh, two can definitely play this game, sweetheart.

After a world-record speed shower, we're only going to be about ten minutes late for brunch. "How come you didn't tell me about going to a party at Bennett Blakely's house?" I ask as we drive down PCH to the Beach Hut for monthly brunch with friends.

"Because I didn't think it was a big deal. I just wanted to go to a party and have fun with my friends. Never in a million years did I think I'd meet Bennett Blakely. And you'll be happy to know I didn't sleep with him."

"Only because there was a damn tiger attack at his house."

"Totally beside the point. By the way, how is the girl who was bitten?"

"She should be fine. Are you going to see him again?" I'm not going to let her change the subject.

"Actually, we're going to lunch tomorrow."

"Would you have slept with him if you weren't interrupted by a tiger bite?" I continue with my barrage of questions.

"None of your business. Now, come on. We're already late." Joey jumps out as soon as I pull into the parking spot.

Pushing past the crowd of people, we find our friends, already seated and waiting.

"Finally you two make it," our friend Michael shouts from across the table.

"Sorry, you know how much of a girl Adam is when it comes to getting ready," Joey retorts.

"No problem. It's given us time to interrogate the new woman."

Oh shit.

At the other end of the table sits Breeann, smack dab between Isabella and Kenzie. Her squinted eyes and pursed lips tell me I'm getting an earful later on tonight.

"Right now, I have more important questions to ask our girl Johana over here." Jessi, Michael's fiancé, shoves her phone in Joey's face. "How do you explain this?"

"Oh my god."

"You're on TMZ with Bennett fucking Blakely. Something you need to tell us?"

Johana's cheeks have flushed ten shades of pink.

"My brother invited us to Bennett's birthday. On a quest to find a bathroom, somehow this lucky bitch stumbles into his bedroom," Isabella interjects.

"His bedroom?" Jessi continues to pry.

"We just took a walk on the beach. Nothing else," Joey explains.

"I don't know. He obviously thinks you're his girl already," I chide.

"Excuse me." Bree pushes her chair back, knocking into the person behind her. "Sorry!" She ducks past the woman and runs toward the front of the restaurant.

"Bree! Breeann!" I hurry after her, careful not to careen into any other unsuspecting patrons. "Babe, stop, please." I grab her arm as we reach the parking lot outside.

She rounds on me. "I'm not stupid, Adam."

"What are you talking about?"

"Every time Johana talks about another guy, the vein in the middle of your forehead starts to bulge."

"What? What are you talking about? No, it doesn't." I rub my forehead, feeling for the vein Bree is talking about.

"I'm only going to ask this once." Breeann squares her shoulders and locks her eyes with mine. "Are you in love with Johana?"

Fuck.

"No. No… I mean… I love her as my best friend, and nothing more. I just want what's best for her." I stumble on my own words.

"Please don't make me look stupid, Adam."

"Bennett! Ben, over here." Shouting is coming from the parking lot.

"Bennett, who is the new girl?"

"Bennett, did the tigers belong to you? Did the girl lose her leg?"

Bennett Blakely exits his convertible Jaguar with a large bouquet of roses and, without saying a word to the paparazzi, heads towards me. I don't even know the guy and I already don't like his pompous saunter.

"Hey, you're the ambulance dude from last night, aren't you?" he asks me.

"Trauma ER nurse. And yes, it was me."

"Thanks. You were a big help." He smacks me on the back before walking inside.

Every muscle in my body tenses; my face burns with anger.

Now I feel the vein Breeann is talking about.

Chapter Nine

Johana

I knew Adam's child girlfriend would make a scene at brunch this morning. I don't know what her deal is but every time she's around there's drama.

"What the hell was that all about?" I ask.

"I think someone's a little jealous," Kenzie teases.

"The question is, who's more jealous, Adam or Breeann?" Bella chimes in.

"Oh, I think we're about to watch Adam's head explode." Kenzie points to the hostess leading the most gorgeous man I've ever laid eyes to our table.

"I couldn't wait until tomorrow to see you," Bennett says, handing me a large bouquet of flowers. "I needed to see you sooner."

"How… How did you find me?" I ask, stammering over my own words.

"I have my ways." He flashes me a smile, already making me want to do bad, bad things to him.

"Would you like to join us?" Bella asks, purposely adding fuel to the fire.

"Miss Johana?" He looks at me with his dark, whiskey-brown eyes, asking my permission.

All I can do is nod like a star-stuck schoolgirl. To be honest, I thought last night was a fluke. I assumed he was saying nice things to me after the fiasco at his party but I never assumed I'd hear from him again.

For the next hour, my friends interrogate him as any normal person would do the first time they meet a celebrity. Who's the best kisser? Who's the worst? Have you ever done a nude scene? Would you?

"Are all the women you've dated as pretty in person as they are in the magazines?" Kenzie asks.

"There's a lot of filters used on those pictures. I've seen much prettier in real life." When his eyes meet mine, my entire body goes hot.

"You ready to go, Joey? I need to get ready for my shift at the hospital this afternoon," Adam interrupts our moment.

"Oh, yeah. I guess. Adam's my ride," I explain to Bennett.

"I've got a car and it's got some nice safety options. Do you think your friend would let me take you home? I bet his girlfriend wouldn't mind," he says loud enough for the entire table to hear.

"Go!" Isabella pushes me into Bennett's broad, muscular chest. "Kenzie and I will stop by Adam's and get your car."

"Adam?" I look at him, waiting for his answer.

"You've said it before, Joey, you can take care of yourself."

"Tell me more about yourself, Joey," Bennett says while driving up PCH.

"Johana or Jo, but not Joey."

"I'm sorry. I heard Adam call you Joey and I just assumed."

"Please, just Johana or Jo.

"How about I just call you sweet lips? Your lips are all I can think about since the first time I kissed you?"

"I like that." I flash a quick smile, thanking him for not pushing the issue.

"So, tell me about yourself, sweet lips."

"Well, I was born in New York. My father is a real estate mogul, and my mother was an Australian model. She died when I was six, and we moved to San Francisco. When my father met his second wife, she insisted we move to Newport Beach, where I gained two monstrous stepsiblings. They divorced my senior year of high school, when Crystal got caught cheating with the food delivery boy. I went to Stanford and earned a master's degree in journalism, met my two best friends and now we all live together as one happy bunch."

"Wow."

"Oh, my goodness. I'm sorry. I just rambled my entire life story." My cheeks flush with embarrassment.

"Don't ever apologize for who you are, Johana." He reaches over, placing his hand on my thigh. "I want to know everything about you."

"I'm sure your life as an actor is much more interesting than mine with the gold-digging stepmom."

"It has its ups and downs."

Pulling up to the aquarium, my eyes light up, a smile stretches from ear to ear, and my hands clap like a kid on Christmas morning.

"I'm guessing you've been here before."

"The Long Beach Aquarium has been one of my favorite places to go since I moved to Southern California. I have a fascination with penguins. Once I was old enough, I hopped the bus once a week and made my way up here."

"By yourself?" he asks.

"Usually with Adam. He and I have basically been inseparable since we met in middle school."

"And you're just friends?"

"Just friends," I assure him. "Now, are we going to the aquarium or are we just going to sit in the car and talk?"

"I wouldn't mind keeping you all to myself but I have a feeling you're more eager to see little furry guys all dressed up in their tuxes."

"Oh, there's something about a man in a suit." I wiggle my eyebrows in a bad attempt to flirt.

"For our next date, I'll have to take you somewhere elegant." Bennett's confidence is sexy. He comes around to my side of the car, holding his hand out, taking control of mine.

"Next date? So, is this our first?" I ask.

"I hope so because I'd love to kiss those sweet lips again."

Damn. This guy is smooth.

Walking toward the aquarium, a small crowd forms around us. The closer we get to the entrance, the more they block our path.

"Mr. Blakely, I've been a huge fan for as long as I can remember. Can I have a picture with you?"

"Sure," Bennett politely obliges.

"Will you take it?" The lady shoves her phone in my hand and has her paws all over Bennett before I can even object.

I take a few shots, quickly handing the over-zealous fan back her phone. Bennett wraps his strong arm around my waist, ushering me inside.

"I'm sorry. Something I've just gotten used to over the years. But I promise you it won't happen again today."

How can he make such a promise? We barely made it to the entrance without being mobbed. What makes him think it won't happen on a busy Sunday afternoon?

"Mr. Blakely. Miss Warner." An older man holds out his hand to greet us. "Welcome to Long Beach Aquarium. My name is Bill and I will be your behind-the-scenes tour guide today. Ready to begin?"

"Of course," I squeal. I wrap my arm around Bennett's and bounce through the doors Bill is holding open for us.

For the next two hours, Bill leads us through the aquarium, showing us things very few get to see. They allow us to feed seals, pet the otters and play with penguins.

"This is where my tour ends. Please continue viewing and page me when you're ready to leave. Thank you again for the donation, Mr. Blakely." Bill nods and walks away.

"Donation, huh?" I giggle.

"I had to do something to impress the girl I'd like to take out on a real date."

"Seriously, how did you pull this off so quickly?"

"After your friends were done playing twenty questions with me, I listened to you and Kenzie talk about the piece you're working on about the changes in whale migration. I text my assistant and ask her to put this together. Plus, it doesn't hurt Bill is her uncle, which is why I kept you talking in the car. I was waiting for the greenlight."

"Thank you." Standing on the tips of my toes, I stretch to softly kiss his cheek. "Would it be okay if we stopped by the gift shop before we left?"

"The aquarium closed fifteen minutes ago."

"Bummer. I have a thing for gift shops."

"Good thing they've left it open just for you, sweet lips."

"Seriously? They don't have to. I'm sure these employees want to go home, not wait for me to pick out some silly snow globe."

"Snow globe, huh? If a snow globe is what you want, a snow globe is what you shall get," Bennett declares.

"Thank you." I smile.

This summer has sucked. Adam left for Hawaii with no warning, Royce is off jet-setting through Europe, and Jimmy dumped me as soon as I said I wouldn't have sex with him. For the last two months, I've only come out of my room when my dad was giving me driving lessons. Occasionally, when Crystal leaves with the kids, I like to sneak down to the kitchen and watch our chef, Nelly, cook.

"You like to cook?" she asks with a European accent as I'm poking around the kitchen."

"I do. My mother and I used to cook together when I was little."

"Crystal used to cook?"

"Oh god, no. Crystal isn't my mother. My mother was killed in a car crash when I was six. She was a model from Australia. Even though I was young, she was starting to teach me how to cook some food from her home country."

"Did you like it?" she asks.

"I did."

"Well, you're in luck, little one. It just so happens, I lived in Australia for six years with my ex-husband. I'm going to teach you the recipes your mother would want you to know."

"Really?"

"Really. I'll even teach you how to make my famous Lamingtons."

The last time my nana came to visit, she brought a box of Lamingtons for my mother because they were her favorite treat as a kid. The moist butter cake squares dipped in chocolate and rolled in desiccated coconut are heaven on a plate.

"Johana!" Crystal screams my name down the hall. I ignore her hollering in hopes she'll leave me alone.

I consider making a run for it, but the wrath of Crystal not finding me may be worse than if she does. "I'm right here. You don't need to yell."

"It's my house. I'll do whatever I damn well please. I have yoga. Take Luna and Lincoln to their playdate," she demands.

"Where's their nanny?" I ask.

"She quit. Something about the kids being uncontrollable. Blah, blah, blah. So, you need to take them."

"Fine." It's not like I have anything else to do anyway. "Who is it with?"

"Mandi, next door. Just take them over there at three and pick them up at five. Can handle it?"

"I feel bad for her mom," I mumble under my breath.

"Excuse me?"

"I said I'll get the job done."

Twenty minutes later, I'm walking my step-siblings to their playdate with Adam's younger sister. It's strange going over there and not seeing Adam. This is the longest we've gone without talking since we met three years ago.

Walking up to the back gate, I recognize the laugh of my friend Royce. What the hell is she doing here?

"A summer in Hawaii did you well, Adam," she says.

What? Adam is back too? Both my best friends are back and neither one has called me? And why are they together? Adam and Royce can't stand each other.

"Surfing every day was a good workout. For my body and my mind." Is he flirting with her?

"Did you get a tattoo?" Royce asks.

"Yeah, but don't tell anyone. My uncle got it for me on my sixteenth birthday."

"It's super sexy. Hey, would you like to go with me to the end of summer bonfire?" Royce asks.

What the ever-loving hell is going on?

"Can we go in now?" Luna asks loud enough for anyone in a half mile range to hear her.

With nothing else to do, I open the gate and the twins take off running toward the house.

Damn. Royce was right. Hawaii was good for Adam. He's grown taller, his dark blonde hair is long, his skin the color of delicious caramel, and beautiful muscles in places there was nothing before.

"Johana! I was just on my way to see you." Royce runs towards me, giving me a hug. "Come on. We have so much to catch up on." Grabbing my hand, she pulls me from Adam's yard and over to mine.

For a solid thirty minutes, Royce rattles on about her summer in Europe, barely stopping for a breath. I nod and smile, but honestly the only thing I can think about is Adam. Why didn't he call me when he got home? Is he still so mad at me? Could he be interested in Royce? Does she like him?

"Hello? Earth to Jo! Are you there?"

"Sorry. What were you saying?"

"I asked you if you talked to Adam this summer?"

"Not once. I tried but he kept his cell turned off. He was pissed at me after the Jimmy thing."

"OMG! How are you and Jimmy? Are you guys officially a couple?"

"No. He dumped me when I wouldn't have sex with him on our first date."

"Why wouldn't you? I mean, he's the hottest guy in school."

"Seriously? I wasn't going to lose my virginity in the back of some guy's '97 Honda."

"Why not? It's where I lost mine." She seriously did not just say that.

"I gotta go get my brother and sister."

"Hey," Adam says as I enter his yard.

"Hey."

"How's Jimmy?"

"Seriously, Adam? This is how we're starting this? I need to get my siblings home."

Like two little tumbleweeds, my brother and sister come barreling through the backdoor.

"Look, Sissy. I found a box with your name on it." Lincoln hands me a small box with my name beautifully written on it.

"Is this for me?" I ask.

Adam just nods.

"Should I open it?"

He shrugs.

"Bye!" Luna takes off out the back gates and starts running toward our house.

"I gotta go." I grab Linc with one hand and the box with the other and take off after her. Her fast legs are no match for me.

I take the box to the privacy of my room before opening. I read the note before looking at the item carefully wrapped in tissue paper.

Joey,

I've been in Hawaii a month trying to forget the fight we had the night before I left. I was doing pretty good until I came across this on one of my uncle's many flea market hunts. It reminded me of our first Ferris Wheel ride. I know it's not as nice as the ones your mother gave you, but I hope you like it.

Adam

I unwrap the tissue paper to see an old snow globe with a Ferris Wheel inside. The wood base is old and starting to splinter in some areas; the red seats on the wheel are faded with age; and the snow still falls perfectly.

I never told Adam the globes I received from my mother were all antiques. She believed older pieces had more sentimental value with meaning attached. Somehow, I think Adam understands that. And me.

"What about this one?" Bennett asks, pointing to a large globe kept behind a locked glass case. The base is gold and the fish have diamonds for eyes.

"Oh, I don't need anything expensive. Something small is fine."

"I insist. It's just as beautiful as you."

Bennett's large hand sweeps my hair back, taking a firm grip of my neck. His other arm wraps around my body, pulling me against his. Running his fingers through my hair, he draws his lips to mine.

Our lips brush, barely touching, but the spark is undeniable. Needing to taste him again, my tongue invades his mouth, taking full control of our kiss. My hands slip into his shirt and up his chest, enjoying each rippling muscle.

Bill clears his throat to get our attention. "Have you made your decision, Mr. Blakely."

"This one here on top." He points to the one with the gold base. "Beauty to only match hers.

Chapter Ten

Adam

Sitting on the toilet, I glare at the magazine staring back at me. My best friend's face is

not what I like to see looking back at me as I'm trying to take my morning shit. The headline on this week's *Hollywood Juice* reads:

Who is Bennett's New Arm Candy?

New arm candy? Joey is so much more than arm candy. Fuck. Now I need to read it.

Who is this yummy piece of candy on the arm of Hollywood's Bennett Blakely? The new pair were spotted Sunday afternoon at the Long Beach Aquarium.
Sources revealed the blonde beauty is Johana Warner, daughter of Australian model and actress Charlotte Taylor. Taylor was tragically killed in a car crash when Johana was only six years old. Warner, 28, is a freelance writer with works published in Yummy Tummy Magazine and High Vibes Weekly.
Will this juicy gumdrop melt her way into Bennett's heart or will she be just another flavor of the week?

The article is followed by several pictures of Joey and Bennett getting close at the aquarium a few weeks ago. Since her break-up with Ian, Joey's been on a rebound hook-up spree. The last thing she needs is her childhood heartthrob fucking with her heart.

Bree knocks. "You almost done in there? I have to shower before work."

I slip out, closing the door behind me. "You might want to give it a minute before you go in."

"I grew up with three brothers and one bathroom. You can't scare me, Crawford." She reaches up and kisses me before entering.

"Don't say I didn't warn you." I laugh.

"Damn, dude! No more Mexican food for you," Bree shouts from behind the door.

I pour a cup of coffee with hopes it will make the pounding in my head disappear.

"Adam?" my girlfriend shouts.

"What's up, babe?" I ask, peeking my head in the steamy bathroom.

"Will you wash my back?" She bats her big eyes at me and I know what Bree really wants.

"Of course." I take a large swig of my coffee and take the soap from her small hands.

"What's wrong?" she asks.

"Just a headache. Too many margaritas with your friends last night." I lather the soap in my hands, preparing to rub every inch of her petite hourglass figure.

My hands start massaging her shoulders, thumbs gently moving to her neck. Slowly making my way down, I take care of Bree's body.

"I think my front side needs to be taken care of also." She spins around giving me access to her perfect breasts.

"Damn. You are so beautiful." My hands slide down her sides stopping on her perfect, hourglass waist.

"Too many margaritas, huh?" Breeann runs her finger down the middle of my forehead, tracing the bulging vein.

"I need to avoid reading *Hollywood Juice* for a while." I nod my head toward the magazine rack.

"Done. Time to switch to *Cosmo.* I need to start reading those 25 Ways to Please Your Man articles anyways."

"Baby, you know exactly what it takes to please me."

Breeann drops to her knees, pulls my gym shorts down to my ankles exposing my already bulging erection. By the time she's done, all the neighbors know she knows exactly how to please me.

“Thanks for coming with me,” Joey says.

“You act like I wasn’t invited,” I tease.

“Still, thank you. I’m only going because these brats are my siblings.”

“They are your stepsiblings and your dad divorced Crystal three years ago. Why are we even going?”

“Just because they’re brats doesn’t mean I still don’t love them to death. And I’m dying to see Mandi, all cute and pregnant.”

“Don’t remind me.” I groan. My twenty-one-year-old sister is three months pregnant.

“You know, technically this baby makes us family,” she says. “My step-brother knocked up your sister, which makes us aunt and uncle in-laws.”

“I think you’re stretching it a bit.” I laugh as her forehead wrinkles, trying to figure it all out in her head.

“So how come Mr. Wonderful isn’t accompanying you to tonight’s soiree?” I ask.

“The twins’ birthday wasn’t the right place to introduce him to the family. Plus, he’s in Canada filming another Christmas movie. And where’s the little tart?”

“Working. Little tart?” I chuckle.

“I thought you might slap me if I called her the hoe of the month.”

“You’re right. I would have. I like Bree. I’m thinking I may keep her around for a while. What is it about her you don’t like?”

“I never like anyone you date,” Joey admits.

“True, but you are particularly salty about Breeann.”

“There’s just something about her. Maybe it was meeting her half naked in *my* bed.”

“Yeah, not my proudest moment. Way too many birthday tequila shots with you.”

“Oh, don’t blame me for this one. Let’s just blame Ian.” She laughs. A laugh I’ve always loved; a laugh which always makes me smile; a laugh I’ll never get tired of hearing. “Why don’t you bring her over for dinner this week and I’ll give her a proper Johana welcome party?”

“Will you be inviting Bennett? Make it a double welcoming.”

Her eyebrow raises in suspicion.

“What are you not ready to introduce Mr. Hollywood yet?”

"I'll see what I can do. Now, let's go party with the kids."

The Uber driver drops us off at the front of the club. Joey bounds up the stairs to the front door of Hollywood's famous Ringer Room. Tonight, we celebrate the twenty-second birthday of the twins by watching Lincoln's band, *The Bettie Wites,* headline their first show

"Jo!" Mandi and Luna run up, grab her by the hand, and drag her on the dancefloor.

Holy shit. My sister has gotten huge since the last time I've seen her. Mandi looks like she's hiding a beach ball in the tiny dress she's wearing. I still can't believe my baby sister is having a child before me.

After being ignored by my sister and ditched by my date, I hit the bar, grab myself a beer and scan the room for anyone I know. Surprisingly, Mr. Warner, Joey's dad, is camped out in a corner booth. He spots me, waving me over.

"Hey, Mr. Warner. Good to see you." I extend my hand to his.

"Adam. Just the man I wanted to see. Please sit."

"You wanted to see me?" I question. Joey's dad and I have always had an interesting relationship. He has always seemed to like me but gets upset with me whenever Joey fucks up. Like I'm her babysitter.

"Tell me, what do you know about this Bennett Blakely guy Johana is dating?"

"Honestly, I've only seen them together twice. The night they met and the morning after."

"The morning after!" Mr. Warner shouts louder than the music.

"I meant at brunch. Bennett tracked her down and surprised her with a date."

"I wasn't thrilled to see my daughter's face plastered all over the tabloids in the supermarket line." I considered telling him about my experience this morning but thought better of it.

"You need to talk to her about this, sir." A chug down the rest of my beer and join Joey on the dance floor, leaving the awkward conversation.

Moving my body in closer with hers, I lean in and say, "We're going to need a lot of shots to get through tonight."

"Why?"

"Because your dad is asking all kinds of questions about you and Bennett."

"My fucking dad is here?"

I point to his table.

"Then I guess we never leave the dance floor because I am so not ready for that conversation."

Fuck. I hate dancing. But I'll do anything for Joey. I always have.

I've been dancing for the last hour straight. I hate dancing. But for Joey I will do anything to see her smile. Junior prom has been going strong for the last couple hours and no one seems ready to stop. When the D.J. slows down the music, Joey and I look at each other and shrug.

Having no idea what to do with my hands, I awkwardly place both on her hips. She places hers around my neck, pulling her body closer to mine. "Thank you for rescuing me tonight. I seriously can't believe Cody got the flu." Joey has been dating the captain of the baseball team for the past few months and was supposed to be here with him tonight.

"It's what best friends do, right?" Plus, I didn't have a date.

"I don't know what I would do without you, Adam."

"You'll never have to worry about that. I'll always be right here by your side, Johana." She places her head on my shoulder and relaxes her body into mine. I want to relax but the growing boner in my pants is saying, nope, it's time to party.

"Hey! Are you two coming to the after party?" a friend asks us as the song ends.

"You want to?" I ask. She bites her lip in contemplation. Damn, this girl is killing me. Joey nods.

"Okay, we all have rooms at The Newport Sands Hotel." She dances off with her date.

"Rooms?" Joey questions.

"We don't have to go if you don't want to. I'll make an excuse to get out of it."

"No, I want to."

"Cool." I shuffle my feet with the music.

"Cool," she repeats. "Come on, I need water." She pulls me off the dance floor, quickly changing the subject.

Using my father's Black Card, I was able to book our room without question. One of the privileges of coming from Newport Beach money. Unfortunately, the only room left was the king suite. But from the sound of the parties already happening, I don't think anyone is planning on sleeping.

"Holy shit! This room is gorgeous!" Joey says, opening the door to our room. "This must have cost a fortune."

"Dad told me to have fun tonight." I laugh.

"And fun we'll have. I just got a text from Royce. Everyone's down in her room."

"Really? There's no other room?" Royce and I went out on one date and honestly, she's everything I hate in girls. She's still pissed I never asked her out again.

"She's dating James Cooper now; he graduated last year and now goes to FIDM to be a fashion designer."

"Huh? I always thought he was gay."

"I think he is, but don't tell Royce I said that." She giggles knowing I'm right. "Now, let's go have some fun."

The hotel was overrun with kids from Balboa High School, music blasting from each room, the smell of pot heavy in the air, and alcohol everywhere.

"Promise not to freak out?" Royce comes running to Joey as soon as we walk into her room.

"Umm. No. What's going on?" Joey asks.

"I heard Cody is here with Tabitha McFarlane. Zoey said she saw him downstairs going into a room with him. Were you guys planning on staying here tonight?"

"I told him I didn't want to because I'm not ready."

"Girl, you need to get over yourself because I think it just cost you your boyfriend."

Joey grabs the beer from Royce's hand and finishes it with one swig. "Which room?" she asks.

"322."

Before I can stop her, Joey is bolting down the stairs to find the room. Pounding on the door, she screams his name with no answer from the other side. It only takes a few minutes for a gathering crowd; the door opens to Cody and Tabitha standing in front of us in nothing but their underwear.

"What the fuck is going on, Cody? I thought you were sick," Joey's voice cracks as she screams at her boyfriend.

"I am sick. Sick of you not putting out. Three months. A guy has needs," Cody says. "Unlike you, Tabitha knows how to take care of those needs."

"Yeah, you and the rest of the entire baseball team. And the football team and I believe the wrestlers too." The collective gasp from the gathering crowd makes me chuckle.

"Fuck you, bitch," Cody yells back. No one said he was a smart guy.

"You tried and failed. So, who's the bitch now asshole? Oh, and if I were you, I'd go get tested for STDs. Tabitha's been passing those around since the eighth grade."

The crowd around us erupts in cheers. Joey storms off without ever giving Cody a second look.

It's close to four in the morning when we stumble back in the room, falling in a mess of limbs on the giant bed.

"Thanks for coming to my rescue again tonight. You always seem to be there when I need you."

"I've told you a thousand times, I will always be here for you. It's what best friends do. I'm sorry about Cody," I say, even though I'm really not.

"Me too. I thought he was going to be the one. I feel like I'm the last virgin at Balboa High School."

"You know you're not."

Joey rolls over and lays her head on my chest, looking directly at me with those gorgeous blue eyes. "I want my first time to be something special with someone special. But I don't want to go to college as a virgin. Do you?"

Fuck. I haven't thought about it. "I guess not."

"Let's make a pact right now. If neither one of us has lost our virginity by senior prom, we'll be each other's firsts. What do you think?"

What the fuck did Joey just say?

"Sure. Okay."

"Thanks, Adam. I know you'll always be there for me." She snuggles her body into mine and drifts off to sleep.

Joey and I stumble up the stairs to my apartment, barely making it in the front door. In avoidance of her father, we spent the entire evening on the dance floor or at the bar.

"I need water," she says, tripping over my running shoes on the way to the kitchen.

"Grab me one, too. I'm gonna change."

Coming out of the bathroom, Joey has already made herself comfortable in my bed.

She slipped out of her dress and found her way into one of my old college shirts. Her long blonde hair draped over my pillow, curvy ass peeking out from under my shirt, and gorgeous legs I've dreamt around my body so many times.

Fuck. This is why I hate being drunk and alone with Joey.

I plop myself down next to her, grabbing the water off the nightstand. "Bree's going flip when she smells your perfume in my bed." I chuckle, reminding myself I do have a girlfriend.

"So? I was here first. Bitch better know her place."

I find it hysterical when Joey tries to get tough. Poor girl has never been in a fight her whole life. "Simmer down there, killer."

"Do you remember the first time we shared a bed together?" she asks.

"Of course I do. Junior prom, 2009. Probably one of the greatest nights of my life."

"Remember the silly pact we made? Do you think we'd still be friends if we'd gone through with it?"

"I don't know. Maybe. I think we'd be good together." Fuck. What the hell did I just say?

"Huh?"

"Nothing. Let's just get some sleep."

"'Kay," she quietly mumbles. Her fingertips run down my arm and find their way into my hand. Our fingers fumble their way around each other, sliding together in a tight hold.

Chapter Eleven

Johana

"What the fuck is going on here?" I'm startled awake by the shrill scream of Breeann. "One night. One night without me and you end up in bed with another woman!"

"Bree. Stop. It's just Joey," Adam says, rolling out of bed. He walks over, kisses her on the forehead before disappearing into the bathroom.

Leaving Bree and I alone in the room.

"I hate you. You don't want Adam, but you don't want him to be happy with anyone else." She storms out of the room, slamming the bedroom door, but not the front door, so I know there's more to come.

"What is her deal?" I ask Adam upon his reemergence.

"She's pissed. Bree is already not too fond of our relationship, and now she walks in and finds us in bed together. How would Bennett feel walking in and seeing us in bed together?"

"Good point. I wasn't even thinking about them last night when we passed out. I'll call an Uber and then apologize before I leave."

"Thanks." He leaves the room without looking back at me.

Grabbing my phone to call for a ride, I see ten missed calls and texts from my dad and my roommates.

Dad: *I'm coming over and you better be there.*

Isabella: *You need to get home. Your dad is here.*

Kenzie: *Girl. Get home, your dad is asking me questions. You know I can't lie.*

Isabella: *Your dad is HOT. Get home or I may do something bad.*

Fuck, what is up with my dad? I request a car and I'm in luck. There's one just seven minutes away. Just enough time to get dressed, apologize, and get the hell out here.

Embarrassed, knowing I should have slept on the couch or just gone home, I creep from Adam's room to face Bree. "Woman to woman, I'm sorry. I overstepped the friendship boundaries last night by not respecting how you would feel. I'd be pissed if I came in and found Bennett in bed with someone else, even if it was his best friend. So, to make amends, dinner this week?"

"I'd like that." Bree smiles and nods.

"Thanks," Adam whispers, giving me a hug goodbye.

"My dad's waiting at my house. Call me later." The text from the driver saves me from any further conversation.

As soon as I'm in the car, I call Isabella. "What is going on?"

"I have no idea. He's been here for the last hour and a half and he says he won't leave until he talks to you."

"He was at the twins' birthday party last night. Adam said he wanted to talk to me, and I avoided him by staying on the dance floor."

"Why are you avoiding your dad?"

"I haven't told him I'm dating Bennett. He found out in the tabloids"

"Oh, someone's in trouble," she teases. "I wish I could get in trouble with your dad. He's getting hotter with age."

"Ew, enough. I'll be home in ten."

My father has to be upset with me if he's made an unannounced visit from New York. Especially showing up at the twins' birthday party last night, risking seeing Crystal. Their divorce was messy and so were the three after her.

"Walk of shame, I see," my dad says as soon as I open my front door.

"You're kidding, right? You watched me leave with Adam. I crashed at his place."

"If you knew I was there, why didn't you come talk to me?"

"I was there to enjoy the twins' birthday, not to hear about your latest marriage."

"Is that why you think I'm here?" he asks. I know it's not but I somehow hope we can change the subject from me to him. "Can we go somewhere private and talk?"

"Yeah."

We take a seat on the patio overlooking the Pacific Ocean. His tired, droopy eyes and wrinkled forehead show a different side to the strong, confident man I'm used to seeing.

"I'm worried about you, princess."

"Me? I'm fine. I'm in good health, my job is going great and I'm dating a man who makes me happy. There's no reason to be worried."

"Okay, maybe I'm worried about me. You're all I've got. When I see my daughter's face plastered across every gossip magazine, every horrible memory comes flashing back. Can you imagine what it felt like to see the same people who killed your mother now after you?"

"I'm sorry. I… I never thought about it. Do you want me to stop seeing Bennett?" I ask.

"Does he make you happy?"

I nod.

"Then no, but I want to meet him. I need him to know how precious my little girl is to me. I'll be in town for two weeks."

"I think we can make dinner happen. So, no new marriage proposals to pop on me?"

"Nah. No more marriages for me. I think I'll just find some little young thing to have fun with," he jokes.

"Gross, Dad."

Isabella pops her head out the door. "Hey, Jo. Hi, Mr. Warner. I'm heading to the store. Do you need anything?"

"No. I'm good. Thanks." She runs off as quickly as she came in.

"Is Bella single these days?" my dad asks.

"Stay away from my friends, Dad!"

He kisses me on the forehead. "I'll see myself out, princess. Call me this week."

I understand where my dad is coming from. Losing my mother was the worst thing that could have happened to him. To us. It still haunts me like it was yesterday.

"Just one game, please, Nana." I bat my eyelashes at her. It works on my parents. Why not my grandmother?

"Your mother said I needed to have you in bed by eight. It's a school night."

"You're only here for one more week and I love spending time with you."

"All right, one more game of checkers and then it's off to bed, young lady."

For the next thirty minutes, we laugh and play as my grandmother tells me about my mother growing up. When we're done, she tucks me in and sings me the same lullaby my mother sings me every night.

Several hours later, I woke up from a repeated ringing of the doorbell. My grandmother and I meet in the hallway.

"Go back to bed, sweetie," she says. "I'm sure your parents just forgot their keys."

Something is wrong. I can feel it. I don't listen to my grandmother. My feet are firmly planted on the ground.

"Ms. Taylor?" a man asks as she answers the door. "I'm Officer DeMarco and this is my partner, Officer Benitez. May we come in?"

"Of course. Is everything okay?"

"I'm afraid not, ma'am. There's been an accident this evening. I'm afraid your daughter didn't make it."

"No!" I scream from the upstairs hallway. "You're lying!" I run downstairs and hit the officer with all the might my little six-year-old fist could muster.

"I'm so sorry, sweetheart." The officer hugs me tight through my fit of rage and confusion.

"And my son-in-law?" my grandmother asks.

"He is in the hospital. He's in serious but stable condition. We can take you to him if you'd like," Officer Benitez says.

"Yes, please." Her warm eyes make me feel safe. I take her hand and my Nana takes the other and we silently walk to the patrol car.

The fifteen-minute drive to the hospital is silent. I need my Daddy.

Hand in hand, Officer Benitez leads me to my dad's room. I run to his side and burst out in tears.

"Don't cry, princess," he says. "I will always be here for you. I promise."

"But mommy?" I say between sobs.

"She's our guardian angel now. Climb up here and cuddle me to sleep. I need princess hugs." I crawl in bed with my dad, laying my head on his chest. We both cry each other to sleep.

The twinkling lights on the oceanfront patio catch my eye as we make our way into the kitchen. The music playing in the background is loud enough to be heard but not a distraction. And whatever Bennett has cooking is making my mouth water.

"Wine?" he asks.

"Yes, please. Anything white will be fine."

"Excellent. I believe I have a couple bottles of Chardonnay left in here." He pulls out a bottle of Louis Jadot and pours me a glass.

"I have not had Louis Jadot since high school," I say slowly, savoring the first magnificent sip.

"Wow. A sophisticated drinker, from a young age."

"No. Just a sneaky kid, trying to piss off her stepmother. I had no idea they were for my father's dinner party or how expensive they were. My friends and I drank three thousand dollars of wine in one weekend."

"He must have been pissed." Bennett chuckles at my antics.

"Yeah, I didn't get to leave my room for a couple months."

"I'd like to be locked in a room with you for a couple months." Bennett lifts me onto the counter as if I'm weightless, positioning himself between my legs. "I've missed these lips."

He gently places kisses along my bottom lip. His strong hand wraps around my neck, creating a deeper bond between us. My hands find their way under Bennett's shirt and along his perfectly sculpted six-pack abs.

"I've missed you, too," I whisper against his lips.

"I'm sorry I had to leave so soon after we met, but you have to admit some of those phone calls were sexy as hell. I'm all yours for the next month, sweet lips. No filming, no appearances, no parties."

"Maybe we should go get locked in a room somewhere together."

"Your wish is my command," he whispers.

I toss my legs around his waist, crashing my mouth on his. Bennett carries me over to the couch, positioning me perfectly in his lap. "Hopefully, my living room will work for now," he whispers as he places kisses on my neck.

"We could be in a closet for all I care, as long as you keep kissing me right here." I point to a spot just below my ear.

He moans as the kisses continue. "So, this is your sweet spot?"

"Yes." My legs clinch tighter around his waist.

"What about here?" Bennett moves his kisses to my collar bone.

"Lower." He grabs the ends of my t-shirt, pulling it off over my head. I do the same to his.

Bennett begins moving his kisses down my chest. "Your heart is racing. Are you nervous?"

"Excited." He reaches around to unhook my bra and we are rudely interrupted by the screeching sound of the smoke detector.

"Shit! I forgot about the bread. He kisses me hard on the lips before running to the kitchen to save the burning bread.

"Soup's good, salad is fine, but the bread is toast," he jokes. "Hey, hey, hey. Don't you dare put your shirt back on." He runs over to stop me.

"Bennett, we're going to eat. We should put our shirts back on."

"Nope. I'm more inclined to eat a good dinner if I'm tempted with dessert." His hands move up my torso, grabbing two handfuls of both my tits, and plants a kiss on me like I'm the best thing he's ever tasted. "Now, let's eat."

A moan unintentionally escapes my lips as the lobster bisque tickles my taste buds. The smooth, creaminess of the soup is something to savor.

"God, I love it when you moan." Bennett's voice has a deep sensual growl.

"I love the things you put in my mouth to make me moan." My hands quickly cover my face in embarrassment.

"You're funny, too." Bennett leans over the table, pulls my hands away from my face and softly kisses my lips.

Breaking our connection, I stand up to unhook my bra and let it fall to the floor in front of me. I straddle his lap, placing kisses on his neck. Bennett's strong arms wrap around me, pulling our half-naked bodies together for the first time.

"You are so fucking beautiful."

I lean back, giving Bennett full access to my tits.

Lifting me up, Bennett carries me in his bedroom, carefully laying me down on the bed. He slides my jeans and panties down, leaving me naked and feeling vulnerable. My natural instinct is to cover up my body.

"Don't you dare hide this luscious body I've been dreaming about since the night we met. I plan on devouring every inch of you from head to toe." Bennett pulls off his jeans, standing before me rock hard in all his muscular glory.

"Damn. How did I get so lucky?"

"I've been asking myself the same question." He cages over me, kissing my breasts, my neck, my mouth. When the tip of his cock brushes against my wetness, he moans. "You're so wet. Are you ready, beautiful?"

"I'm so fucking ready."

Bennett reaches into the nightstand drawer and grabs a condom. In one swift motion, he rips the package open and slides it on. He leans in, kissing me as if he's dying of thirst and I'm his saving drink of water. Our hands link together above my head. Bennett takes his time filling me with his impressive girth; his only concern is taking care of me.

Over the next several hours, Bennett and I enjoy taking care of each other over and over again.

"I was serious about getting lost with you. Maybe not for a month, but how about for a week or so," he says, playing with my hair as I lay on his chest.

"Sounds wonderful," I sigh.

"Why does your sigh tell me otherwise? Is it too soon? We don't have to go anywhere. I just want to spend time with you, getting to know you, with no distractions."

"I want the same thing."

"But?" he questions.

"My dad saw our date at the aquarium in the tabloids and he's worried," I explain.

"Oh shit. I had no idea. I avoid those magazines like the plague. But I don't understand why he'd be worried. I'd never let anything happen to you, Johana."

"He used to stay the same thing to her." I sit up, pulling the sheets over my naked body.

Bennett looks at me puzzled. "This may require another bottle of wine."

Bennett grabs the bottle and our glasses from the kitchen and quickly returns to bed. I'm already fighting back tears and I haven't even begun to relive the memory of the worst night of my life.

He sits against the headboard, directing me to sit in front of him. As Bennett wraps his strong arms around me, I feel safe. For the first time, I may be able to get through this story without crying.

"Now, sweet lips, tell me what has you so sad and your dad worried about us."

"My mother was Charlotte Taylor."

"Why does that name sound so familiar?" he asks.

"Eighteen years ago, she was killed in a car crash after leaving her first U.S. movie premiere. She wasn't feeling well and wanted to avoid the paparazzi. My father shielded her as they waited for the valet to bring their car. A couple of photographers spotted her and swarmed her in an attempt to get an interview. When my parents left, they were followed. He didn't want to lead them to our home, so he started making random turns, attempting to lose them. A chase began."

I pause for a moment, taking a long sip of my wine. As I'm telling the story of my mother, it hits me like a ton of bricks why my father is worried about me.

Bennett begins gently kissing my shoulder, moving his way up to my ear. "I will never let anything happen to you. I promise," he whispers.

"You can't make that promise. My dad promised the same thing to my mom. They ended up on Mulholland Highway. It was pouring down rain, he took a curve too fast and they went over a cliff. My mother died before they could be rescued. My father was in the hospital for several weeks. I didn't find out until I was much older that the reason she wasn't feeling well was because she was pregnant."

"Oh, baby. I'm so sorry." His arms squeeze me tighter.

"It was a long time ago. But my father would like to meet you. Are you willing?"

"If it means I get to keep dating you, I'll do anything."

Chapter Twelve

Adam

Nights like these at the hospital can drag on forever. Today was the annual Turtle Boat Surf Championship in Newport Beach. My entire shift has been one drunk person after the next. Most just need a bottle of water and a few hours to sober up, but a good old-fashioned stomach pumping usually prevents repeat offenders.

"Hey, Crawford. Go check out the hottie in room two. Ass is smokin'," one of the interns leans over the desk and whispers to me.

"Seriously, man? This poor girl is drunk and you're telling me to go check her out. Unprofessional, O'Grady."

"She's not one of the party goers. Girl fell off a ladder and her ankle looks like a baseball. And you should go check her out because she's your patient."

"You're an asshole." I laugh, grab her chart, and head off down the hall. When I see her name, my feet take off in a sprint.

"Joey? What happened? Are you okay?" I ask, throwing back the curtain.

"Look at you, trying to be all superhero like," Isabella teases.

"Bite me, Boobs for Brains." For as long as I've known Bella, we've had a playful banter between us.

"Careful what you wish for, her last boyfriend said her jaw has a strong grip," Joey joins in.

"What did you do?" I remember I'm at work, turning my attention to Johana my patient and not Joey my friend.

"I was hanging lanterns on the patio for this weekend's dinner. A seagull swooped down to steal a chip off the table. And, well, you know my fear of birds. I screamed, scaring the bird enough to fly off and hit me in the head. Hence, screaming like a maniac and falling off the step ladder."

"What have I told you about you and ladders?" I ask.

"Stay off of them because I'm clumsier than a person with two left feet."

"You never listen to me and now look at you. We'll take some x-rays, but by the looks of it, you just have a mild sprain. A week or two of staying off of it and you'll be back to normal."

"I'm gonna do everything I can to make sure this ankle is better before I go to Kauai in two weeks," Joey says.

"Kauai?" I question. Who the hell is my Joey going to Kauai with? Why haven't I heard about this before?

"Bennett and I thought it would be nice to get away for a week. He's got a place on the south side of the island and wants to take me there."

"Are you sure that's a good idea? What does your father say about this?"

"Seriously?" Isabella questions. "I don't think it's your—or her father's—business who Jo dates. She and Bennett are good together and your jealous ass needs to mind its own business."

"Sorry, I'm just trying to protect her from ending up like her mother," I spit back before I can even stop myself from saying it.

Isabella's jaw drops.

"Adam, enough. Can we just get my ankle fixed up so I can go home?"

"Yeah. Of course." I step out of the room, embarrassed by my behavior.

"Why did you say that?" I hear Joey ask Isabella while I'm still in earshot. "You know as well as I do, Adam is not jealous of my relationship with Bennett."

"Girl, you are as oblivious as you are clumsy."

Why is it Bella can see right through me but Joey can't?

"Nurse Crawford, how's our patient this evening." Dr. Greene loudly greets me from behind. Fuck, now Joey and Isabella know I heard their conversation.

"Just a mild sprain, doctor. Should be an easy fix. I'll have one of the interns wrap her up."

Bennett rushes past me and into Joey's room. Of course, he'd be here running to her rescue. Something about him just gets under my skin.

Driving home, I stop at the liquor store on the corner, grabbing a pack of cigarettes and a small bottle of whiskey. Smoking isn't a norm for me, but something about taking a long drag of the nicotine calms my mind.

Fuck. Breeann is here. I told myself giving her a key was going to bite me in the ass. Honestly, a needy girlfriend is the last thing I want to deal with tonight. I just wanted to smoke a few cigarettes, take a couple shots, and pass the fuck out.

I'm so angry at myself for making the comment about Joey ending up like her mother. But goddamn, the thought of losing her the same way she lost her mother kills me.

I take a large swig of whiskey straight from the bottle.

Then there's Bennett Blakely. Perfect specimen of man. How do you compete with the guy who is number one on most women's—and possibly men's—celebrity cheat lists?

The whiskey burns the back of my throat as I swallow an even larger drink than before.

Now Bennett is whisking Joey off to Kauai. Kauai is our place. I took Joey there for the first time. It was me who showed her the local spots. Those are our sunsets and now she wants to share them with him.

I take a few long drags off the cigarette, attempting to force my mind out of overdrive. Two more swigs from the bottle and it's gone and I'm drunk. I'm not much of a drinker so it doesn't take much these days.

How could Joey not know how I feel? After all these years—over half our lives—and she's never noticed how I look at her? Doesn't she realize I'd do anything for her? She has to know. Nobody can be that oblivious to love, can they?

She knows. She's known since the seventh grade. Joey will always keep me in the friend zone because I let her keep me there. I need to stop living in the fantasy believing things will change between us and just forget about Johana Warner.

I catch my reflection in the rearview mirror of my Jeep. I'm a good-looking guy. I may be a bit drunk at the moment, but I'd do me. You know who else would do me? My hot girlfriend in my apartment.

I stumble my way up the stairs, barely able to get the key in the door. The moment I kick the door shut; I strip down to nothing but my boxers.

"Bree? Are you here?" I call out. No response.

"Breeann, Breeann, where could my little woman be?" I singsong through the house quite loudly.

In my bed, I find my stunning girlfriend asleep. Every inch of her naked body, screaming to be touched by me. As any other red-blooded male would do, I took advantage of the opportunity in front of me, tangling our bodies up in pure aggressive pleasure.

"Damn, baby," she says, rolling over, running her fingers along my chest. "I didn't know you had a rough side to you."

"Neither did I." I chuckle. "Sorry. Guess I was a bit more wound up after work than I thought."

"Don't apologize. I liked it when you smacked my ass and pulled my hair."

"Something I'll remember for next time." I lean over and kiss her full, sweet lips.

"Rough night at work?" Bree asks.

"Yeah, a couple patients threw me for a loop and the new intern drives me up a wall."

"Good thing I was here to relieve your tension."

"My body is still filled with tension. I think you need to climb on top and relieve me all over again."

Cars line Joey's street as far as the eye can see, including every side street throughout her entire neighborhood.

"Looks like someone is having a kick ass party," Bree says from the passenger side of my Jeep.

"Well, by the looks of it, our dinner has turned into a dinner party." Why does this not surprise me? Joey avoids anything remotely uncomfortable by surrounding herself with a ton of friends.

"What the hell, Adam? I'm not dressed for a party. I thought it was just dinner. You need to take me home so I can change!"

"You look amazing. You already changed five times before we left because it had to be the right outfit for meeting Bennett. If I take you home, we'll be over an hour late. And I pride myself as a person who's never late. To anything."

"Whatever." Her attitude is starting to annoy me.

"Are you seriously mad about this?"

"Of course, I am."

Fuck, I thought she was joking.

"I'm sorry, I'm just not going to drive another hour and miss half the party so you can change for the umpteenth time today. I don't understand what more people being here has to do with the outfit you're wearing.

"You just don't get it," she mumbles under her breath.

"Are you trying to start a fight?" I pull in the driveway, throwing the car in park.

"Let's just get this over with." She slams the door of the Jeep and heads into the party before me, then storms past Joey and her roommates and locks herself in the bathroom.

"What's the tart's problem?"

"I need to talk to you." I grab Joey's arm and pull her into the kitchen.

"Ow! What the hell, Adam?" She yanks her arm away from me.

"This was supposed to be a small dinner so you and Bree could get to know each other, not a full-blown party."

"Who gives a shit, Adam? I decided to throw a party. You and my dad both want to get to know Bennett. I'm being forced to get to know what's her name. And why is she being all bitchy anyway?"

"She said she's not dressed properly for a party."

"That's the dumbest thing I've ever heard. What does she think this is, high school? I've told you, Adam, to stop dating children."

"A child? Why don't you tell me how you really feel?" Breeann stands in the doorway of the kitchen.

"Bree, I'm… I'm sorry," Joey stutters.

"Yeah, somehow I don't believe you. You had no intention of getting to know me, did you?" Joey wants to answer, but Bree gives her no chance. "And riddle me this, Batman. Why am I such a child, being six years younger than Adam, but it's okay for you to be five years younger than Bennett?"

"Bree, I'm sorry—"

"Damn right you are! You don't want Adam, but you don't want him to be with anybody else either. I make him happy and there isn't anything you can do to mess us up."

"Is everything alright?" Bennett interrupts the girls' argument, which is making me much more excited than it should.

Joey slowly picks her jaw up from the floor, taken aback by Bree standing up to her.

"Your dad is asking for you. Shall we?" He puts his hand on the small of Joey's back leading her from the kitchen.

"Are you okay?" I ask Bree, pulling her into my arms.

"No. No, Adam, I'm not okay." She pushes me back. "Johana is never going to give me a chance."

"She will. Just let me talk to her."

"It won't make a difference. One day, you're going to have to choose between her and the woman you love. And I hope for your sake, you make the right decision."

"I hope that is a decision I never have to make. Can we forget about this fight with Joey and start the night over? There's someone here I'd like for you to meet."

"One of Johana's friends?" she asks sarcastically.

"Come on." I link my fingers in hers and start my search.

Three rooms later, I spot the pint-sized beach ball at the food table with a plate full of goodies.

"I should have known this is where I'd find you."

"Adam! Come sit with me. I can't be on these swollen ankles a minute longer."

I follow Mandi to the table where she has staked her claim on this evening. Without even looking up to see us, my sister begins shoving her mouth with food.

"Slow down there, Turbo," I tease.

"I'm eating for two, ya know," she says with a mouth full of fruit. "Oh, hello." After being together for close to ten minutes, my sister finally realizes we have company.

"Mandi, I'd like you to meet my girlfriend Breeann. Breeann, this is my little sister, Amanda."

"Girlfriend? Oh, I got questions." She stands up, pushing me with her belly. "Move over. I want to sit next to my new sister-in-law."

Her comment is perfectly timed with a long swig off my beer. I choke, spitting my drink all over me and the table.

"I'll just go get a towel." I leave before anything more can be said.

Chapter Thirteen

Johana

"Why does Breeann have to cause a scene everywhere she goes?" I whine, walking away with Bennett.

"Why do you let her get to you? Was she right about you not wanting Adam to be happy with anyone else?"

"Absolutely not. I want Adam to be happy. I just don't think Bree is the girl for him."

"She could be."

I brush off Bennett's last comment as we sit down at the table with my dad.

"Hey, princess. I have to run. Early showing in the morning in the Pacific Palisades. But I wanted to tell you, after talking to Bennett and expressing my concerns, I feel like you're in good hands."

"I could have told you that, Daddy."

"Told him what?" Adam comes up from behind and joins our conversation.

"I'm in good hands with Bennett."

"I bet," he mumbles under his breath. The scowl on his face is obvious to everyone at the table.

What the hell is Adam's problem? Does he have a problem with me and Bennett?

"I'm looking forward to getting away and spending time in Kauai," I say, changing the subject.

"I remember how excited you were the first time you got to go to Kauai. I don't think I have ever seen you smile so big," my dad says before standing up, kissing me on the top of the head as he always has, and leaving us to finish this conversation.

"You didn't tell me you've been before," says Bennett.

"Yeah, Adam and I went after we graduated high school for a few weeks."

"I had an uncle who lived in Hanalei. I used to visit him during the summer. It was the best present I could offer Joey at the time."

"Why don't you and Bree come with us?" Bennett asks.

"What?" Adam and I blurt out simultaneously.

"It would be a great opportunity for us all to get to know each other. The ladies' relationship had a rocky start, and I would like to get to know you better since you are my girlfriend's best friend. So, what better way to do it than a week in Kauai?"

"Don't you think you should have talked to me about this?" I ask.

"I'm just not sure what Bree and I can afford at the moment."

"Don't even worry about it, bud. I've already chartered a private plane and we're staying at a friend's place to ensure privacy. It's all on me."

I can see the vein of frustration popping out on Adam's forehead. Knowing him as well as I do, he hates when he's called out about money. Adam's always had a great job but doesn't spend money frivolously. Quick jaunts to Kauai on private jets are not something he'd ever do. He would plan for months to find the cheapest deals and lowest bargains.

"He was just offering for you to join us because there's enough room for everyone." I put my hand on his arm, attempting to control his temper or to stop him from saying something stupid.

"I'll talk to Bree. Thank you for the invite," Adam says stoically.

"I'm gonna go grab another beer. Anyone want anything?" Bennett asks.

"I'd love another Jack and Coke, please."

"Anything for you, beautiful." He leans down, kissing my lips softly.

Every time this gorgeous man I've fantasized over almost my entire life touches me, I sit in awe, still trying to convince myself this is all real.

"What the ever-loving fuck?" Adam quickly brings me back to reality as soon as Bennett is out of earshot.

"What?"

"Seriously? Do you actually want Breeann and I in Kauai with you on your romantic getaway?"

"I'll admit, at first I was shocked by Bennett asking you to join us, but even though I don't always act like it, I want to get to know Bree. I know she's important to you. And I think I might be falling in love, so I would like for you and Bennett to be friends."

"I'll try. You know I'd do anything to see you happy, Johana."

"That's why you're my best friend." I pull him into the hug that always makes me feel warm and comfortable.

Bree walks up, clearing her throat to make us aware of her presence.

"We were just talking about you." Adam lets go of me and reaches for her. "Bennett has invited us to go to Kauai with him and Joey next week."

"Really?" she raises an eyebrow in question.

"Really," I say. "If Adam is this smitten with you, I would like to get to know you better. I am sorry for the way I've treated you in the past and would love for this trip to be our olive branch."

Bennett returns, handing me my drink. "So, are we making this trip a foursome?"

I give Adam a reassuring nod.

He sighs. "If I can get my shifts covered at the hospital, we're in."

"Great. Just let me know by mid-week so I can make arrangements. Now, if you don't mind, I'd like to take my girlfriend on a walk."

Bennett's strong fingers slide into mine as he leads me down to the sand. So many thoughts are running through my mind, but not a single word will come from my mouth.

"You're quiet, sweet lips."

"Tonight was a lot."

"It was, but it went well. I enjoyed meeting your dad. He even invited me to play golf with him when we return from vacation."

"Thank you for appeasing him. I'm sure meeting fathers isn't something a huge television star like you is used to doing."

"First of all, you need to stop thinking of me as Bennett Blakely the soap star and start thinking of me as Bennett Blakely, the guy who's falling for you. And if meeting your father was something I needed to do for you to be my girlfriend, then by all means I'm meeting your father. His concerns are justified after what happened to your mother."

Even with the moon being the only light in the sky, I feel like my cheeks are burning from the heat of a thousand suns. I bury my face in Bennett's chest, with hopes he won't notice.

"Why do you blush like a cute little strawberry every time I say the word girlfriend?" he asks.

"I didn't realize we were official." My voice is barely louder than a whisper.

"Are you dating anyone else?"

I shake my head no.

"Do you want to?"

Same response.

"Since the moment I met you, you're all I've been able to think about."

"Seriously? You've been shooting a movie with Cameron Howell—America's Christmas movie sweetheart—and you're telling me I was all you could think about." I chuckle in spite of myself.

"Cameron doesn't hold a candle to you, Johana. These sweet lips—" He leans down kissing me softly. "Have captivated me from the first second I laid mine upon them. I want to claim them for myself. So, yeah, I want to make this official. Johana Warner, will you be my girlfriend?"

I jump up, wrap my legs around his waist, and crash my mouth onto Bennett's. I grab handfuls of his thick brown hair, forcing a deeper connection. "Yes," I whisper upon his lips.

"I think we need to cool off. Are you up for it?" He raises one eyebrow in question. Still in shock, I'm barely able to nod.

We both look around. Not a person in sight. Never letting go of me, Bennett reaches down, unbuttons his shorts, sliding them down with ease. Knowing he has a grip on me, which will never let me fall, I reach down to pull my sundress over my head.

"You are one of the sexiest women I have ever seen," he says with a growl in his voice, making my panties wet before we ever step foot in the ocean.

Never letting me go, Bennett inches his way into the water; our bodies adjusting to the cold water. My body shivers when chilled by the cold breeze.

"Cold?" he asks.

I nod.

"Let me warm you up." Bennett pulls my body in tight before crashing his lips against mine. Despite the cold wind, a heat rages through my body; a desire I can't and don't want to control.

His massive erection presses against my stomach. "See what you do to me?"

"I seem to have a positive effect on you." I giggle. "Maybe we should take care of that?"

"Here?" Bennett seems shocked by my suggestion.

"Sorry." My head lowers in embarrassment.

"Why are you sorry?"

"I know it would be a bad career move if someone saw us."

"Oh, baby, I could care less if someone sees us. Okay, not entirely true, but that's not why. We're in the middle of the ocean. I don't keep a spare condom in my boxers."

"I have an IUD and you can pull out." A smile creeps from the sides of my lips.

"You are a bad girl, Johana Warner."

"I can be." Knowing Bennett has a tight grip around my waist, I reach down and slide his boxers off his perfectly sculpted ass. On my way back up, I slide my bikini bottoms to the side.

"You sure?" he asks.

I grip his broad shoulders, using them as leverage to hoist myself up to the tip of his cock. Slowly, I slide down, allowing Bennett to completely fill me. Together, we ride each wave of pleasure, until our orgasms leave us exhausted.

I woke up this morning to hot coffee and breakfast in bed. He is the first man who has ever taken care of me the morning after. The more time I spend with Bennett, the quicker I am falling for him.

"I see the 'I just got laid grin' plastered across your pretty little face," Bella teases, poking at my cheeks.

"That obvious?"

"Well, he was still here this morning," Kenzie adds.

"I know. Bennett Blakely woke in my bed and made me breakfast in bed. Me! No one has ever done that for me before."

"Adam has," she replies.

"Seriously? Why would you even include him? It would be like saying your sister never cooked you breakfast."

"All I'm saying is he looked upset when you and Bennett took off last night."

"It's probably just because he wants me to spend time with Breeann. But I guess we'll get to know each other in Kauai."

"What the hell are you talking about?" Bella shouts. I explain to my roommates about Bennett inviting Adam and Bree on our getaway.

"How do you think this is going to go?" Kenzie asks.

"It's going to be good. Bennett and I are falling for each other and Adam and Bree are serious, so it's only right for us all to get to know each other. Right?"

"You keep telling yourself that, sweetheart."

"Enough you two. It's going to be fine. Adam and I have been best friends since we were kids. And that's how it will always be. This trip to Kauai will be good for all of us. Now, today is about Jessi and her bridal shower. Let's go enjoy her day."

Throughout the party, the conversation from the car weighs heavily on my mind. Are my friends, right? Is this trip a dumpster fire waiting to happen? I mean, how well do I honestly know Bennett? And Adam always makes sure I'm safe. I do want to get to know Bree. I think.

I wander down the hall of Jessi and Michael's home, looking at the pictures of the amazing life they are building together. Since I was a little girl, this was all I ever wanted. A quiet life. A great husband, a few kids, and a big backyard overlooking the Pacific Ocean.

"Piece of cake for your thoughts?" Jessi sneaks up behind.

"I'm so happy for you, friend. You and Michael are going to have a wonderful life together."

"Thank you, but I know you too well. Spill it."

"Bennett invited Adam and Bree with us to Kauai and the girls were giving me a hard time about it on the way here. They think it's a bad idea."

"What do you think?" she asks.

"Adam is my best friend. Bennett is the man I'm falling in love with. I want them to be friends. And Adam says he wants me to be friends with Bree. So, if we're all friends, it will be a good thing."
"I think you answered your own question."

Did I? Because truthfully, I feel more confused than ever.

"Time to wrap our bride-to-be in a toilet paper wedding dress," Jessi's sister informs us.

"Seriously?" My friend has a look of fear in her eyes.

"Come on. We'll get through it together." I laugh.

Linking arms, we join the party, forgetting any worries of my upcoming trip.

I've finished my article on whale migration ten days early so I would have nothing to worry about while on vacation. Plus, it's given me an excuse to avoid my roommates for the last few days. But I know my avoidance can only last so long.

"Can we talk?" Bella and Kenzie knock and enter my room at the same time.

"I guess."

"Oh, seriously! You still can't be mad at us?" Bella asks.

"Of course, I can. I've told you both over and over there is nothing between me and Adam. We are friends. That's all."

"Are you trying to convince us or yourself?" she continues.

"There is nothing to convince anyone of. Adam and I have been friends since we were twelve. He knows me better than anyone. Relationships are complicated and messy and more often than not, end badly. And when things end badly, friendships are ruined. I can't risk my friendship with Adam. I won't." Tears burn my eyes. Why won't these two just leave it alone?

Kenzie sits down next to me, wrapping her arm around my shoulder. "I'm sorry. I guess because I'm on the outside looking in, I see something different."

"I'm asking you to stop seeing what you want to see and start looking at the great relationship I'm trying to build with Bennett," I plead.

"Can I ask you something?" Bella asks.

"Sure."

"What's it like to fuck the legendary Dr. Ryan Hope?" She laughs, lightening the mood.

"Honestly, I feel like I am living one of those steamy soap scenes you never want to end."

"I hope your relationship is filled with love and happiness and not ex-wives and relatives coming back from the dead like most daytime dramas," Kenzie says.

"Thanks. I think."

"We just want to see you happy, Johana."

"Adam makes me happy."

"What—?"

"Bennett! Bennett makes me happy."

Shit.

Chapter Fourteen

Adam

What in the hell ever possessed me to say yes to going on this trip? I accepted the fact years ago, Joey and I will never be together, but it doesn't mean I will ever enjoy seeing her with someone else. Now we're headed off to the one place I thought would always be "ours".

"What did you think?" I ask.

"I've never seen anything more beautiful."

"Neither have I."

I know Joey is referring to the aqua blue waters and sparkling sand in front of us, but I still can't take my eyes off her. After two weeks on the island, Johana has never looked more gorgeous. Tan skin, long, gorgeous blonde hair, and blue eyes matching the ocean in front of us.

I need to stop pussy-footing around and just tell Joey how I feel. I've been in love with my best friend since the seventh grade. She must know. I mean she'd have to be blind not to see how I feel.

"What's the plan?" Johana asks. "We only have a couple days left here and I want to do something wild."

"Wild, huh?"

"Not up for it, Mr. Goody-Two Shoes?" she teases.

"Oh, I'm up for any adventure with you, my dear Joey. Go get dressed. We're going out."

"What? You already made plans for us?"

"I did. I know you better than anyone, Joey. I want to make our last night here one you won't forget. Now go get dressed and we'll leave in about an hour."

She leans over and kisses my cheek. "Thank you for this vacation and for being my best friend. I don't know what I'd do without you."

Johana practically bounces into the house to change for our evening out. I've arranged everything to the T for the night to go perfectly. I'm going to make our first time a night she won't ever forget.

Ninety minutes later, Joey emerges from her room looking like someone I've never seen before. "Holy shit," I say louder than I intend to.

"What? Is this not okay for what we're doing?" she asks.

"It's perfect. You look amazing." The skintight Hawaiian print dress hugs her body perfectly. And her tits. Damn, her tits are gorgeous. Now, I have the extra challenge of hiding my boner from her all night.

"So, is your uncle driving us?" When we came to the island, my uncle insisted we did not need to rent a car. What I didn't know is he was insistent to drive us everywhere we went. I know he was just showing us island hospitality, but it has really been a cock-blocker. But not tonight.

"Nope. Surprise number one. Look outside."

"Oh, please tell me the convertible Jeep out there is ours."

"Ready for an adventure? I have a night planned we will never forget."

I open her door, helping her in the car.

"What a gentleman." She giggles. I'm going to do everything I can tonight to show Joey just how perfect we can be together.

As soon as the car leaves the driveway, Joey flicks the radio on and cranks the volume all the way up. Feverishly, she changes the station, looking for something she likes. And of all songs, she lands on "Dirrty" by Christina Aguilera. Listening to her sing along to these dirty lyrics is causing things to stir in places I try to avoid.

Pulling into the Grand Hyatt Resort, Joey gives the single raised eyebrow with her cute little smirk. "A hotel?" she questions.

"They have a great restaurant," I reply, with my own coy smirk.

"Checking in?" The valet asks as I exit the Jeep.

"Yes. Under Crawford. Adam Crawford."

Out of the corner of my eye, I see Joey's expression turn from excited to worried, which is not what I was hoping for.

"You okay?" I ask, putting my hand on the small of her back and guiding her into the resort.

"We're staying the night here? I thought we were just having dinner?"

"This is one of the most beautiful places I've been to on the island and I wanted to spend an evening here with the most beautiful girl I know."

"Who? Where is this creature of beauty? I must meet her."

"You're such an idiot," I tease. "Honestly, I was tired of us being under my uncle's watch. We only have a few more days here before we go back to California, and

then we're off to college. So, will you, Miss Joey Warner, accompany me for two days of eating, sleeping in, and lying on one of the most beautiful beaches in the world?"

"Are you sure your beautiful girl won't mind?" she teases.

"I think she'll understand I can't leave my best friend out in the cold. Now, come, or we'll miss dinner reservations."

With Johana, small talk has always come naturally, but tonight I can't seem to form two words together to make any conversation. I want to tell her how beautiful she is. I want to tell her I've been in love with her since the seventh grade. I want to tell her I want us to be each other's first before we go to college.

I have replayed the night of junior prom over many times in my head. I turned down more dates than I should have this year, holding out for my chance to be with Johana. She never told me she lost her virginity this year, so maybe she's waiting for me too.

"You're quiet tonight. What gives?"

I thought I was being cool about it, but I guess not.

"I can't help but think about college. Everything's going to change in three weeks. It will be the first time in six years, I won't see you every day."

"Stanford and UCLA are only five and a half hours apart. We'll see each other all the time, I'm sure. Now, stop being a party-pooper. We're here to enjoy ourselves. I wish I would have known we were coming here; I would have brought my bathing suit. The hot tub over there is calling my name."

"Good thing I thought of everything. Let's go get changed and hit the hot tub."

It took all of thirty minutes for us to change, find fruity non-alcoholic drinks and secure a private nook in one of the resort's many hot tubs. Joey sits next to me with her legs stretched out over mine. Unconsciously, my fingers run up and down her tan thighs.

"So…" I drag the o out longer than I should.

"So?"

"Do you remember our deal we made after junior prom?"

"I do." Even in the dim light I see her cheeks flush crimson red.

"Are you?"

"Adam." Her voice cracks.

"You did? When? With whom? And why didn't you tell me?" My heart breaks a little more with each question. As much as I think I want to know, the answers are truly going to kill me.

"It… It just happened one night when I was at a college party with Royce," she stammers.

"Seriously? I've held out all year in hopes my first time would be something special. With someone special."

"Why would you do that? I never asked you to wait for me."

"Sometimes, I just can't be with you, Joey." I get out of the hot tub and leave her there alone.

Breeann bounces around her apartment, packing more suitcases than she could possibly need. At last count she has packed twelve different swimsuits. I don't even own twelve pairs of shorts.

"I still can't believe we are actually going to Kauai with Bennett fucking Blakely. When I told my sister, she flipped out with jealousy and begged me to take her with me."

"You could take her instead of me. You sound more excited about spending time with Bennett than me anyways."

"Stop being stupid. Of course I want to spend time with you. But you have to admit going with a celebrity is fucking cool. I wonder if we'll get the celebrity treatment. My Instagram following is going to double after this trip."

Bree and I are only six years apart, but at times it feels like she's light years away. I couldn't care less about Bennett's celebrity status. What I do care about is how his celebrity status is going to affect Joey. And more than anything, I despise social media. Don't have it, don't need it, and definitely don't want it. Bree insists she only has it for work; more pictures of her ass mean more likes, which in turn gets her paid. Still doesn't make any sense to me.

Bree wraps her arms around me from behind, pulling me close to her. "I'm sorry, babe. I am totally looking forward to spending time with you. I'm just hoping the exposure of being with Bennett will get me off the phone screens and onto the big screens."

"You do realize soap stars aren't very well-known actors, right?" I ask.

"It's cute you think that. When you're the only person to land on *People Magazine*'s sexiest men alive list for five consecutive years, you kind of become a big deal."

Fuck, how did I not know this? I like this fucking guy even less now. How am I ever supposed to compete with the sexiest man alive? I'm not. He has Joey and I have Bree and we are both perfectly happy.

Bree slides her away around, bringing her face to mine. She reaches up softly, placing kisses along my jawline. "Bennett's good looking and famous, but you, you save lives. Nothing is hotter than a man who saves lives." Her kisses begin to devour my mouth. I want to return the action with the same fervor she's giving, but it just feels forced.

By some stroke of luck, we're interrupted by the honking of Joey here to take us to the airport.

The adventure begins.

Landing at the Lihue airport, I realize it's been over a decade since I've been to Kauai. For most, the island is a dream vacation, a place of relaxation and enjoyment. For me, it is a place of sadness and things I'd rather forget. I'm hoping this trip can turn this around.

"You were practically silent the entire flight. What gives?" Joey asks, bumping into me as we wait for our luggage to be unloaded.

"You and Bree seemed to be getting along and I didn't want to interrupt such a rare occurrence."

"Eh, she's growing on me. It's been a long time since we've been to the island."

"Ten years. I haven't wanted to come back." I look up from my shuffling feet to meet Johana's striking blue eyes. I can't pull myself away from the grasp of her stare. I want to, but my body physically won't let me.

"You two look way too serious for our first day in paradise!" Bree runs over, jumping on Adam's back.

"Cars are ready!" Bennett shouts, signaling us over. "I got us each a Jeep, so we can take off and explore the island on our own."

"Awesome. Ready to get lost in a jungle and do some things on our own, if you know what I mean," Bree says, wiggling her eyebrows.

Joey's louder than expected chuckle causes us all to turn in question.

"Something funny?" I ask.

"Oh, I know exactly what Bree means, and the thought of you being so risqué is hysterical. You are way too much of a prude to do the nasty outdoors."

"Like you ever have."

"Twice," Joey retorts.

"In one night," Bennett adds.

"I could have gone my whole life and been just fine not knowing that."

"Yeah, but I bet now you're curious," Joey says, hopping into Bennett's Jeep.

"Not in the least." Fuck, when did this happen? How come I've never heard about it? It's like she says these things because she knows they're going to get to me.

Chapter Fifteen

Johana

Kauai is one of my favorite places in the world. I've only been here once, but I think about my trip here often. What would have happened if Adam and I had made love? Would we still have gone our separate ways in college? Our entire lives have taken a different path by just the change one decision could have made.

Lihue is the second largest city in Kauai and is not much different than most small towns on the mainland. Driving south to Koloa, the paradise I remember returns to view. Lush green trees, taller than all of us combined, flowers from every color of the rainbow, and ocean water bluer than any sky I've ever seen.

"Thank you." I lean over and kiss Bennett on the cheek.

"For what?"

"All of this. This is so amazing. And for inviting Adam and Breeann. Our first getaway together and bringing Adam and his girlfriend, probably isn't what you had in mind."

"To be fair, I invited your friends."

"Well, it was really sweet of you."

"I'm falling for you, Johana Warner. I'm falling fast and I'm definitely falling hard." Every inch of my body tingles hearing Bennett say he's falling for me. I feel the need to pinch myself to make sure this isn't a dream. "I know Adam is a huge part of your life, so I need to try to get to know him better. Just like you should with Bree."

"I love everything you said up until the last part." Tingles gone.

"Johana, you need to give her more of a chance. She's kind of a cool chick."

"She's a child!" I retort, because honestly, it's the only reason I can think of at the moment to not like her.

"I could say the same about you," he teases.

"Now you're just being mean."

"Give her a chance. For Adam. And for us. Otherwise, it's going to be a long ten days. Here we are. Home for the next week and a half," he says, pulling a fairly modest house.

"Oh." Shit. My hands cover my mouth trying to shove my comment back in.

"What's wrong, sweet lips?"

"Nothing."

"Not nothing. What is it?"

"I thought we were staying at a hotel or a resort. I was kind of looking forward to room service. And some alone time with you."

"Trust me. This place is much better than a hotel and I have thought of everything."

"Are we at the right place?" Adam startles me by popping up by the car window.

"Yes, we are, man. Welcome to paradise. Let's go grab some drinks and I'll show you around."

When Bennett opens the door to let us in, my jaw drops. The house is much larger than I expected. I'm instantly drawn to the floor to ceiling windows, overlooking the backyard including an oceanfront pool with a private beach.

"I seriously think I've died and gone to heaven. This view is incredible!" I step out on the lanai and breathe in the fresh ocean air.

"Isn't your condo right on the beach?" Bree asks.

"Yes, but it's Southern California, so it's usually filled with smog and skater kids. Definitely not the same." I laugh.

Bennett wraps his arms around me from behind. "No skater kids here. The beach is shared only by the other houses on the street. The neighbors value privacy as much as we do. The house next door belongs to Aolani Ho, number one female surfer in the world right now, and on the end of the street is retired football player Richard Grovanski and his family."

"Who does this house belong to?" Bree asks.

"Cameron Howell."

"Have you been here before with her?" I ask.

"We've vacationed here a few times in the last couple years when we needed to escape the cold of the set in Canada."

I wiggle myself from Bennett's hold. Why does Cameron Howell bring out the jealousy monster in me?

"Where are those drinks you mentioned? I could use a glass of wine."

"Why don't you ladies slip into something more comfortable. I'll have the chef prepare some food and Adam and I will choose a few bottles for wine to celebrate our first evening here in Kauai."

"Chef?" Bree asks.

"Of course. We have a bartender, chef, butler, housekeeper, and massage therapist on staff. I want this to be the most carefree and relaxing trip any of us have ever had. Now seriously, go put on some swimsuits and let's have a good time tonight."

The master bedroom is just as spectacular as the rest of the house. The four-post bed, in the center of the room is draped with a white lace canopy and adorned with the perfect amount of twinkle lights is every girl's fantasy.

Just as in the living room, the bedroom has large floor to ceiling windows except for the French doors leading to a private deck and staircase leading to the beach. Listening to the waves crash on the shore, I take in each sound as if it's something I've never heard before. Why does the ocean sound more beautiful on the island?

My bliss is interrupted with a knock at my bedroom door. "Miss Warner?"

"Yes?" I open with slight hesitation.

"These are from Mr. Blakely." The gentleman presents me with a glass of champagne and an eloquently wrapped box with a note.

Like an excited child on her birthday, I rip open the gift before even opening the card. A bikini? A very skimpy bikini. I don't wear things unable to cover this curvy ass.

The note is written as beautifully as the box was wrapped.

Johana,
Last month, I was flipping through a magazine one of the extras left on set.
When I saw this bikini all I could think about for the rest of the day is how incredibly sexy your body will look in it.
I may have a hard time keeping my hands off each delicious curve.
Bennett

What the hell? Here goes nothing. I slip out of the sundress I've been traveling in all day and into the pieces of triangle cloth connected by a piece of floss. I fix my hair and make-up and do a double take in the mirror.

I have always been too modest to wear something which shows my entire ass, but knowing Bennett picked this out for me makes me feel sexy as hell. The triangle top holds my double Ds in with the perfect amount of under boob peeking out.

As sexy as I feel, I still don't have the confidence to traipse around the house with my ass exposed to everyone. I throw on a cover-up I brought, and join the others already partaking in drinks.

"I hope one of those is for me." I slide into the seat next to Bennett.

"Of course," he says, handing me a glass of wine. "You didn't like your gift?"

"I love it." I slide my cover-up to the side, giving him a glimpse of what is underneath. "I'm just not comfortable walking around with my ass on display."

"You should be. It's a gorgeous fucking ass." He leans closer, gently kissing my lips. "I mean, I seriously considered buying you a wardrobe of assless clothes to wear on this trip. Just so I could stare at it any time I want."

"I knew it." I chuckle. "You only want me for my luscious ass."

"It's not the only reason, but it definitely helps," he teases. "Come on. Let's go join Adam and Bree in the hot tub. It's rude to leave our guests alone."

"Again, you just want to see what's under here."

"Of course, I do. But I'm more looking forward to our time later tonight when you have nothing under there."

"Me too."

Pulling the cover-up up and over my head, I feel Adam's eyes lock on my ass. Fuck, I forgot about Adam.

"Wow."

"What?"

"That's quite a suit you have on there. Not really your style though, is it?"

"Bennett picked it out for me. Makes me feel… sexy." I give a twirl.

"Girl! You need to show off your backside more often. You have a perfect Kardashian ass," Bree adds.

"Thank you. Seems you're the only one here who doesn't appreciate my assets," I tease, giving Adam a boop on the nose before sitting across from him. The scowl he gives in return lets me know how he truly feels.

Bennett refills everyone's wine glass before joining us with his glass raised. "A toast. To new relationships and growing friendships. Here's to an exciting trip to paradise."

"Cheers." We all clink our glasses together.

My eyes connect with Adam's. His eyes are dark and sad. For being in his favorite place on the planet, my best friend isn't happy.

With the champagne hangover from the night before, my stomach flips as the Jeep bounces down the dirt road. I have a death grip on the 'oh shit handle' to keep myself from sliding into Bree's lap. We park on the side of the road next to a large hole in the fence.

"I thought this was a big tourist place. Looks more like private property to me," I say.

"I've been here before," Bennett reassures me. "It's fine."

We grab our backpacks and begin the descent down the path. The red mud trail is wet and slippery, making the hill difficult to get down. Every few feet I have to catch my feet from slipping out from under me. Luckily, between the foliage and Bennett, I always have something to grab on to.

"Yes! I made it down without falling!" I pat myself on the back when stepping off the mud and onto the rock formation.

"You deserve a gold star for that one since you usually can't make it downstairs without falling on your ass."

"Watch it, Crawford, or I may have to knock you on your ass."

"Welcome to Queen's Bath. You guys are in for an amazing adventure today." Since the moment we began planning this trip, Bennett has done nothing but talk about how excited he is to show me his favorite spot on the island.

The rocky coastline is lined with large lava rock pools, cascading waterfalls on side and the Pacific Ocean on the other. I'm in awe of the natural beauty.

We tuck our bags behind some rocks and make our way to the first pool. Bennett races past me and dives in without taking a second look. I, on the other hand, am much more cautious. I need to assess how deep it is, what's below me, and what could potentially bite me.

As the ripples slow from Bennett's dive, the water becomes crystal clear, allowing me to see anything and everything beneath me. The pool is surprisingly much deeper than I thought, relieving my fear of hitting the bottom.

"Jump, sweet lips," Bennett encourages me. "I won't ever let anything happen to you."

Without a second thought, I jump into the pool and swim into the arms of the gorgeous man waiting for me. I wrap my legs around his waist and pull my body close to his.

"This is amazing. I feel like I'm swimming in one of the great wonders of the world."

"Just wait. This is just the first in a series of many pools. They go up the coast for about a mile each one more spectacular than the next. It's a lot of swimming and rock climbing. Are you up for it?"

"I'm up for anything with you." I lean in placing kisses along his strong jaw line; the saltwater makes his taste even more addicting.

Adam clears his throat behind us. Bennett and I are so lost in each other we hadn't even noticed we were joined by Adam and Bree.

"And we're off." Bennett climbs up from the current pool and dives into the next. We follow his lead until we reach the final pool with the spectacular waterfall flowing into it.

"You were right, Bennett. This is one of the most picturesque things I've seen since we've landed."

"I said the same thing when Cameron brought me here for the first time last year."

"Is everything we plan on doing this week something Cameron took you to do first?" I ask.

"Maybe," he says nonchalantly. "I mean she's always been my tour guide and now I get to be yours."

What is about Cameron Howell that makes me so goddamn jealous? Maybe it's her perfect body and gorgeous hair. Maybe it's the fact she's America's sweetheart actress. Or maybe it's that I can't separate acting and reality when she and my boyfriend are kissing. Their chemistry is off the charts; if I get the gooseys watching them, I can only imagine what they are feeling.

After hours of swimming through every pool in Queen's Bath, our bodies are spent. The trek back to our belongings is lengthy; every step on these lava rocks is becoming more difficult.

Bennett and Bree are having no issues, taking the lead on Adam and me.

"We need to start going to the gym more," I say.

"Speak for yourself. I could keep up with your superman if I wanted to."

"Then why don't you?"

"Because someone needs to be back here to look after your clumsy ass," he teases.

"Like I've told you before, I'm a big girl. I can take care of myself." The playful banter I have with Adam is one of my favorite things about us.

"Okay. See ya." Adam takes off to catch up with Bennett and Bree.

He only makes five strides before his feet slip out from under him on a mossy rock. Adam's feet went straight up, with his back and head crashing down on the rocks. He isn't moving.

"Adam fell!" I scream.

Bennett and Bree turn around, running back toward us.

He's only a few steps from me but it feels like an eternity to reach him. "Adam! Wake up! Can you hear me?"

"Head hurts like a bitch. What happened?" He lifts himself up to a sitting position.

"You slipped and hit your head. We need to get you to a hospital."

"I'm fine."

"Adam!" Bree screeches, throwing her body on his, knocking him back over. "Baby! Are you okay?"

"I'm fine. Just a headache. Now, help me stand up." Bennett extends his hand to help Adam up. The second Bennett lets go of him he teeters like a kid who just got off the teacups at Disneyland.

"You do not look fine, brother. Let me help you back." Bennett wraps his arm around Adam's waist, practically carrying him back to where we tucked our towels away.

Adam's eyes are glassy and dazed. I suspect he's more hurt than he's letting on, but being the EMT, I don't want to second guess him when he tells us he's fine.

I hand the first towel to Bree, assuming she'll take it to Adam and make sure he's doing okay. Instead, she wraps the towel around her waist and takes off to watch a group of turtles she spotted in the water.

"Seriously?" I mumble. I hand Bennett his towel and take Adam his, wrapping it around his shoulders.

"You don't look so hot."

"This headache hit me out of nowhere. My head is fucking pounding."

"Well, yeah, you hit your head hard," I remind him.

"I did? When?"

Shit. He doesn't remember. This is not good. "Bennett! Bree! Let's go! We're taking Adam to the hospital."

Reluctantly, I pull Adam to his feet. With Bennett's help, we make it up the steep, muddy path back to the Jeep.

"Joey, when we get back to the house, will you do that thing you do with my pressure points to get rid of this headache?" he asks.

"We're going to the hospital, Adam. This is much more than a headache. You fell."

"I did?"

"You did. Now, get in the car so we can go because you're scaring me."

Adam pulls a pack of cigarettes out of his backpack and lights one up.

"I didn't know you smoked," Bree says with a disgusted look on her face.

"Only when I get these migraines. I need Joey to do her pressure point thing when we get back to the house."

"You hit your head; we're taking you to the hospital. Now, will you put the cigarette out." Bree's voice is like nails on a chalkboard to me. I'm finding it harder and harder to be nice to the child.

"Sorry." He drops the half-smoked stick into an old water bottle.

For three minutes, the car is silent.

Until Adam pulls out another cigarette.

"Sorry, everyone, I only smoke when I get these migraines. I need Joey to do her pressure point thing when we get back to the house."

Bree starts to say something to him but I put my hand on her leg to stop her, shaking my head no. She takes the hint, not finishing what she was saying. Adam only takes a few drags, pushing the remainder into the bottle.

At 1:37P.M. I start watching the clock closely.

Three minutes go by and like clockwork, Adam pulls out another cigarette telling us the same thing he did three minutes ago.

"I can't breathe with all this smoke," Bree whispers. Leave it to Bree to be worried about herself.

"Hey." I put my arm on his shoulder. "You don't have a migraine. You smacked your head extremely hard. I don't think smoking all these cigarettes is good for you or anyone else in the car."

"This is my first one," he retorts.

Bennett holds the water bottle up to show Adam his previous butts. His confused look indicates no recollection of smoking any of the previous cigarettes.

Every three minutes during the forty-five-minute drive to the only hospital on the island, Adam smokes a cigarette, complaining about his sudden migraine.

Walking into the ER, we're all in shock to see an empty waiting room. Being from California, you just expect to see waiting lines for hours. Within minutes of arriving Adam is taken back to meet with doctors.

The minutes seem like hours as we wait for them to tell us anything about Adam's condition.

"Johana Warner?" the nurse calls out finally. "The doctor would like to speak with you." She motions me to follow her.

"I'm going too." Bree follows close behind. "I'm his girlfriend."

"Sorry, miss. Miss Warner is listed as Mr. Crawford's emergency contact. We'll let you know what's going on shortly."

"Why don't you two head back to the house? I'll just call an Uber when we're done." I rush over to kiss Bennett before running off to follow the nurse.

"Miss Warner. Nice to meet you. I'm Dr. Hui. I understand you were with Adam at the time of the fall. Can you please tell me what happened?"

In as much detail as I can I explain the events of the morning to the doctor.

"What worries me is that your story contradicts what Mr. Crawford has told us. He said you pushed him. Is this true?"

"Adam! Why the hell would you say that? You know I didn't push you!"

He's trying so hard not to laugh, but his Muttley, the cartoon dog, laugh is slipping through. "I vaguely remember you saying something about knocking me on my ass. Maybe you did."

"You are such an asshole. No, Dr. Hui, I did not push him. This is just Adam's sick sense of humor."

"Looks like your friend is going to be fine. He has a severe concussion. His memory will come as the swelling goes down. I recommend he take it easy for the next ten days. We'll keep him here to rest for a few hours and then you guys can go home." The doctor closes the door, leaving Adam and I alone.

"You gave me a scare today," I say, crawling in the bed next to him.

"Who are you again?" he teases.

"Asshole. You wish you could forget me." I smack his chest.

"Thanks for being here, Joey. I still don't remember anything about today, but having you next to me now makes this all a little less scary."

I nuzzle my face into Adam's chest, wrapping my arms around him, squeezing tightly. "I was scared, too."

He kisses the top of my head. "You and me against the world, kid."

Chapter Sixteen

Adam

The pounding in my head feels like a jackhammer on a city street. My body feels like I've been in one of the worst fights of my life. By last night, my short-term memory returned, but I still have no recollection of the fall. Or my first cat scan, dammit!

Bree is still sleeping, so I quietly slip out of bed, trying not to disturb her. I pour myself a cup of coffee and join Joey on the oceanfront lounge chairs.

"Well, good morning there, Slippity-Doo-Dah," she teases.

"Ha ha ha. Very funny coming from Miss Two Left Feet over here."

"How are you feeling?"

"I fucking hurt. Everywhere. Thanks for your help yesterday. Even though I don't remember any of it."

"You should be thanking Bennett. He practically carried you from the pools to the car. Without him, I don't know what we would have done."

Seriously? I had to be carried out by Bennett. I would rather not have known. On top of losing my memory, I think I just lost a bit of my pride.

"Hey there, Dances with Lava Rock, how's the noggin?" Bennett joins us from the beach.

"Have you two been sitting around all morning and thinking of smart-ass shit to call me?" I ask.

"Yeah, kinda." Joey laughs. "I can't promise I'm not going to start calling you my little goldfish."

"What? Why a goldfish?"

"Goldfish only have three second memories. You only had a three-minute memory, like a giant goldfish."

"Yeah, it's a big no on that. You know how I feel about fish."

After drying off, Bennett squeezes in behind Joey and my skin crawls. It's different than before. It has nothing to do with Bennett, per se; I'd feel this way if it were *anyone* sitting behind Joey because it's not *me*.

Yesterday was one of the biggest scares of my life. I've lost just one day of memories with Joey and it's killing me. I can't imagine losing a lifetime of memories with her to some other guy. I won't.

Joey's my penguin. Now I need to convince her I'm hers.

"Good morning, everyone." Bree joins us, gently kissing the top of my head before curling up in my lap.

Shit. Bree. In the midst of admitting to myself I'm still in love with Johana, I forgot I have a girlfriend.

"What's the plan for today?" I ask.

"Nothing for you. You have a concussion. The doctor said you need to take it easy for next week."

"I'm only here for a week. No way I'm taking it easy. If it's on the agenda, I'm up for it."

"Seriously? You're a nurse. You know better. Why don't we all just hang out at the beach today? Bree, you said you wanted Bennett to teach you to surf, right?"

"I do. I agree with Johana. Let's just chillax in this bomb ass house for the day. Who knows, maybe you will catch a glimpse of Richard Grovanski."

"Are you a Northeastern Pirates fan?" Bennett asks.

"My dad's from Boston, so our family has always been Pirate fans."

"Well, he happened to shoot me a text yesterday after we got back from the hospital. He and Jade are having a luau this weekend and would love for us to join them."

"That, I am definitely up for," I say, unable to contain my excitement. I may have downplayed my fandom of Richard 'G' Grovanski just a bit. I've got my number 87 jersey on every Sunday, whether it's football season or not. It's bad luck not to.

It's becoming harder not to like Bennett the more time I spend with him. He's a decent guy and the first stand-up guy Joey's dated in forever. Maybe I should just leave well enough alone? Did I have my chance a decade ago and blow it? Should I just step away and let her be happy?

Bree's been surfing on her own for hours now. The girl's a natural. I wonder if this actually was her first time or if she just wanted to say she was taught by Bennett Blakely.

I've spent the entire afternoon thinking about what the hell I'm supposed to do next. The only conclusion I came up with is nothing. At least not yet. We're both in good relationships, but with the wrong people. I need to make her see otherwise or I may lose her forever.

"How ya feeling?" Joey asks.

"Fine. I'm tougher than I look. What would you have done if my memory reset every three minutes for the rest of my life?"

"We'd put you in a home. Just like the guy in 50 First Dates."

"Seriously? A home?"

"What else would I do? I guess, I could build a giant glass aquarium to put you in," she continues to tease.

"What the fuck?"

"Just like a giant goldfish. It wouldn't matter. Your memory would reset and you'd just forget where you are anyways." She busts out into a belly laugh.

"You're such a bitch." I can't help but love her.

"Well, you'll love me again after you see the surprise I have in store for you tomorrow. Get a good night's rest. You and I are going on an adventure."

I look at my watch. "Looky there, it's already past my bedtime. Night all."

Joey's smile makes me want to go anywhere with her. I'd follow her to the center of the Earth if she asked me to.

"You're such a dork. Come on. Let's grab Bennett and Bree from the water so we can finally eat some food."

Bennett has hired one of the most remarkable personal chefs on the island to cook for us for the week. Tonight, he has presented us with a beautifully seared mahi-mahi with a pineapple glaze and coconut rice. This meal looks like it would be served in a five-star restaurant.

Rather than looking at the plate in front of me with culinary delight, all I see is jealousy. Jealous this is a life I'd never be able to give Joey. Bennett has the money to offer her everything she dreams of. I don't have the right to take that away from her.

Rolling over, I smack the shit out of the screeching alarm. Why in the hell does Joey want to leave by five in the morning? After all these years, she should know I am not a morning person. Yet she insisted we needed to be at our destination by 5:45A.M. and not a minute later.

"What's the plan for today?" I ask, jumping in her Jeep.

"Just hold your horses there, cowboy. You'll see." Joey's eyes have a gleam of excitement, but her brow furrows with trepidation.

When we pull up to Ha'ena Beach, I realize why Joey has drug me out of bed so early. The sunrises are some of the most breathtaking views on the island. It was one the places Uncle Nick insisted we see on our trip here a decade ago. It was during that walk Joey told me the entire story of her mother's passing.

"Want to watch the sun rise with me?" she asks.

"Of course." We join hands, interlocking our fingers, and walk to the shoreline.

"It was on this beach I realized you would be my best friend for life. You know you were the only person I could ever talk to about my mom."

"What about Royce? You guys were close."

"No. She never seemed to care when I tried so I stopped trying. You seemed to understand things about her I couldn't explain to others. I like to believe she sent you to me as some kind of guardian angel."

We're both silent for the next few minutes as we watch the sun peek out from the ocean's horizon. The pink and purple clouds against the gentle blue sky makes it feel as if the angels are watching us.

"Do you like Bennett?" Joey asks, interrupting our silence.

"What? Where did that come from?"

"It's just… Do you like him or not, Adam?" I have not had enough coffee for this.

"He's a cool guy and he treats you good, I guess. So, I don't have a reason to dislike him."

"Not really the answer I was looking for."

"Give me a break, Joey. I'm just getting to know the guy. Seriously, what is this all about?"

"I'm falling in love with Bennett. It's been a while since I've had these feelings about anyone. And obviously, the last few times I did I was wrong about them. You told me they were wrong from the start, but you don't say much about Bennett. I just wanted reassurance from you that I wasn't making another mistake before I told him."

Yes! Yes! Yes! I scream internally. *Bennett is the biggest mistake of your life.* But I can't say that to her.

"He seems to make you happy. Are you happy with him?"

"I am. It's hard when he goes away, but we can make it work."

"What happens when Hope's Landing is off hiatus, and he has movies to shoot with Cameron Howell in Canada?" I threw the Cameron thing in there just because I know she gets to Joey.

"Luckily, I have a job where I can travel and work, so I can visit the sets whenever I want."

"Sounds like you have it all worked out then." My tone goes cold, no longer enjoying this incredible sunrise.

"Well, alright, then."

"I'm sorry, Joey. You know I'm not good at talking about relationships. If you think Bennett is the right guy to give you your ranch home with the wrap around porch, three kids, two golden retrievers and a cat named Gizmo, then go for it."

"How do you remember all that shit? I didn't even remember wanting a cat named Gizmo." She laughs.

"When things are important to you, I pay attention. I bet I remember a lot more than you think I do."

"What would I do without you?"

"Forget you wanted a cat named Gizmo," I tease.

"Well, what I haven't forgotten is how much you love moco loco and I know this great little place up the road." Joey holds out her hand helping me up from the seat I've taken in the sand.

"I don't know if I'm ready."

"You'll be fine. I'll be right there with you." Joey's reassurance doesn't make me feel any better. "I talked to Auntie Lani yesterday and she is expecting us."

When the sign for Nick's Loco Shack came into sight, my heart races and my palms begin to sweat. It's been seven years since he's been gone and I still haven't fully accepted it.

"Well look what the cat dragged in," my cousin Niko says from behind the counter of the Shack.

"Adam. Johana." Auntie Lani, Nick's wife, hugs us each respectively, followed by my cousin. "I'm so glad to see you both. Please, come sit. It's been a while." She directs us to what used to be Uncle Nick's favorite booth.

"Auntie, I'm sorry I haven't been back. I let myself believe that if I didn't come back here to see he was gone then he might still be here."

"I understand. Every day I still hope his boat will come sailing into the harbor." Seven years ago, my uncle and his buddy took a sailing trip to San Diego. The trip to California was smooth sailing, but they hit a bad storm on the return trip. Radio contact was lost on the second day and they haven't been seen or heard from since.

"He was the first person in my life who passed away and I didn't handle it well."

"You are here now, which is all that matters. We've missed you very much, Adam. You too, Johana. I'm so happy to see you two are still together. How come you're not staying with us? You know your uncle would be so upset to find out you were staying in a hotel."

"We're actually staying at Cameron Howell's place in Kolona. She's a co-worker of my boyfriends," Joey chimes in.

"Cuz! When you start working with the rich and famous?" Niko asks.

"I'm not her boyfriend. That honor belongs to Bennett Blakely." My aunt raises her eyebrow in question.

"Well, Adam's dating an Instagram model." Joey attempts to deflect.

"She's a Booty's waitress with a couple thousand followers. Is she really considered a model?"

"You're so mean!" Joey jabs her boney elbow into my ribs.

"Ten years later and still fighting like you're an old married couple. Some things never change," Auntie Lani teases. "Are you sure you're not a couple?"

"No," we say simultaneously.

Niko places the largest plate of moco loco I've ever laid eyes on in front of us. Joey and I finish every last morsel while sharing stories and remembering my uncle. I didn't realize I needed this closure until Joey brought me here today.

Morning had turned into afternoon before we say our goodbyes. When giving me a final hug, Auntie squeezes me tight and whispers. Fight for her.

The car ride back to the house is silent. From the sighing under breath, the quiet is driving Joey nuts. She likes to talk. She needs to talk about things until enough people have reassured her she's doing the right thing. My answers about Bennett this morning was not what she was looking for.

I won't lie to her and tell her and tell her she's making the right decision with Bennett. But I still can't tell her the truth about how I'm feeling. This shit is beyond messed up. I need a drink.

Entering the house, I walk directly past Bree and straight to the bar to pour myself a whiskey and Coke.

"No hi, no kiss and straight to the bar. Rough day?" Bree asks, taking the seat in front of me.

"Just a lot," I say, shortly.

"Wanna talk about it?"

"No!" I shout at her. "I just want to sit her and have a drink in peace and fucking quiet." I grab my drink, the half-full whiskey bottle and storm off leaving Bree in my wake.

"Hey, man, you okay? You were a little harsh on Bree back there." Bennett sits down next to me, handing me a cigar.

"Thanks. Rough day. Not something I want to rehash with Bree tonight."

"Take it easy on the girl. She's really into you."

"Yeah, she's a good kid." I take a long swig from the whiskey bottle.

"You're not as into her as she is you, are you?"

I can't answer. Instead, I say, "Don't hurt her," with a drunken arrogance.

"Breeann?"

"Johana. She's the most important person in my life. I'd kill for that woman." I grab the bottle, heading back to the house.

Chapter Seventeen

Johana

Today's the day I'm going to tell Bennett I love him. I think. I know we have strong feelings for each other, but is it love? After Ian, I made myself the promise I wouldn't tell another guy I loved him until I was sure he was the one.

He says he's falling for me, but it doesn't mean he loves me. What if I say it and he doesn't say it back? I couldn't handle it.

"What's going through your beautiful mind, sweet lips?" Bennett asks.

"Nothing much. Just excited to spend a day with just the two of us. It feels like it's been forever since we've been alone."

"It's been three days." He chuckles.

"What can I say, I like having you all to myself."

"I'm all yours, baby. Now let's go have some fun."

I hop in the Jeep, buckle up and put all thoughts of love as far out of my mind as possible.

Bennett Blakely is definitely a man who knows how to pull out all the stops for a woman. Today we took a helicopter tour over the volcanos, had private hula lessons, and got to visit the set of Island Investigators, a new action show Bennett wants to audition for.

"I'm starving. Are you ready to eat?"

"Definitely."

"Excellent. I've made reservations at The Beach House Restaurant."

"Seriously? That's one of the nicest restaurants on the island."

"Have you been there?" he asks.

"No, but when I was food blogging in college it was on my bucket list of places I wanted to eat."

"Yeah, I read that somewhere." He smiles and winks at me.

"Did you read my blog?"

"I did. I want to know everything about you, Johana Warner." My heart flutters with his words. There is no doubt I am falling in love with this man.

Parking the Jeep, Bennett jokingly reminds me to stay in my seat and wait for him to open my door. His gentleman like demeanor has made today all the more special. He opens my door, extends his hand to help me out, and wraps his arm tight around my waist as we walk into the restaurant.

We follow the host through the restaurant and onto a candle lit outside patio overlooking the Pacific Ocean.

"Is this to your satisfaction, Mr. Blakely?" the young gentleman asks.

"Perfect, thank you." He hands us each a menu and quickly scurries off.

My brain is currently on sensory fantasy overload. Taking in everything around me, I feel like I'm the beautiful woman in one of Bennett's movies. The patio is lit by twinkle lights and lanterns with candles allowing the true beauty of a Pacific sunset to be seen. Bunches of bright pink, orange and purple flowers adorn each table giving it the perfect touch of elegance.

"Ready to check out the menu?" Bennett asks.

"No need." I giggle, already knowing exactly what I want. "Seafood linguine, especially with fresh ahi, is one of my favorite dishes on the planet."

"Good to know." His smile makes every inch of my body weak. I lean over the table, softly placing my lips on his. Bennett slides his hand around the back of my neck, deepening our connection.

"Ahem." The waiter interrupts our moment. "Good evening. Are we ready to order?"

"The beautiful lady here will have the seafood linguine; I will have the Furikake dusted ahi which will pair nicely with the Louis Roederer Cristal Champagne."

"Excellent choice, sir. We will have that right out for you," the waiter says before leaving us alone again.

"You know you've got the girl, right? You don't need to impress me with expensive champagne."

"I know I don't, but I like to. I've worked since I was eighteen and I've waited a long time to find someone who gives me the overwhelming desire to share everything I have with you. You do that, Johana. I want to share everything with you."

All right, this is it. If he loves me, this is the moment he should tell me.

"Here is your champagne." The waiter pours us each a glass, interrupting what could have been our moment.

Bennett raises his glass. "To us. Each and every day we spend together, I am falling more in—"

"Oh! My! God! It's Ryan Hope!" A young woman starts screaming and calling all of her friends over to gawk at Bennett like a fish in an aquarium.

The group slowly turns to a small mob as they inch closer to our table. Bennett seems oblivious to it all, yet I can't ignore the whispers from behind getting louder.

Before anyone can intercept, three women in tacky bridesmaids' dresses crash into our table, practically knocking over the champagne. If it weren't for Bennett's quick reflexes, I'd be wearing the $400 bottle rather than sipping on it.

"Aren't you Ryan Hope? From that soap opera show?" slurs the girl with way too much tit and not enough dress.

"I'm Bennett Blakely and yes I play Ryan Hope on Hope's Landing."

"See! I told you." The second girl nudges her with an elbow, practically knocking the poor thing over.

"Would you like an autograph?" Bennett asks.

"No. I have no idea who you are. But my sister is your biggest fan. I mean like huge. Posters on every wall, huge. Like until she met this jerk she just married, she always said she wanted to marry you."

"I'm sorry, but is there a point to all of this?"

"Ask him!" Girl two nudges again.

"Will you come sing some wedding song you sang to some chick on the show you were on? It would be a dream come true for her."

"Not tonight ladies. I'm out with a very special-"

"Your friend can come too," the girl with the big tits says, looking me up and down.

Bennett looks at me to answer. "Go. I'll give Bella a call while waiting for the food."

"I'll be gone for ten minutes. Fifteen tops. You are something else." He leans down to kiss me but is yanked away before we make contact.

My friend answers before the first ring even finishes. "Well, well, well. I was beginning to wonder if you died and went to paradise heaven."

"Not yet, but I may be headed there." I fake a chuckle.

"Dying or being in paradise?" Bella questions.

"Maybe a little of both. I don't know anymore."

"Has Bennett still not told you he loved you?"

"No. He always seems to get interrupted. Tonight's been the worst." By the time I'm done telling Bella about the drunk bridesmaids, I can't tell if we're laughing at me or for me.

"Your dinner is served." The waiter places the exquisite plates in front of me.

"Thank you," I whisper to the waiter, still on the phone with my friend. "I guess I should go and call Bennett and let him know our dinner is here. How long have we been on the phone?"

"Almost twenty-seven minutes. Must be one hell of a wedding. Call me tomorrow and let me know how this all goes down. Good luck, girl."

Just after pressing send, the table vibrates from Bennett's phone. With as quickly as he was yanked out of here, it's no surprise he left his phone behind. He's been gone nearly thirty minutes now. How long am I supposed to wait for him? I've waited the last seven years to taste this bucket list dish, yet the thought of eating it alone has somehow already tainted the flavor.

I FaceTime Adam.

He answers quickly. "Hey. Are you okay? What's wrong? Aren't you with Bennett?"

"I was but he got pulled off to sing at some wedding. I'll tell you all about it later. I just didn't want to eat alone. Are… are you busy with Bree?"

"No. She found some goat yoga class on the beach and I refuse to believe farm animals crawling on your back can be relaxing. And they poop! Have you ever seen how much a goat poops?"

Within seconds, Adam has me laughing, forgetting Bennett has left me alone for some random wedding. For the next half an hour, we ate, drank, and talked all through the small screens on our phones. It was the first time all day, I didn't feel like something was missing.

I'm long finished with my dinner and the entire bottle of champagne by the time Bennett returns. He offered to get us another bottle, but at this point I just want to leave.

"Stop apologizing, Bennett. Things happen. You're a celebrity and people want your attention. I remember it being the same way with my parents." Bennett's been apologizing since he returned. Apparently, the wedding was a bit crazier than he expected. Each time he tried to leave, someone else pulled him over for a picture, an autograph and even a few dances.

Bennett wraps his arm around my waist, spinning me around and bringing us face to face. "Why don't you slip into one of those sexy bikinis we bought you today, I'll pour us some more champagne and will spend the rest of the evening under the stars in the hot tub."

"Sounds perfect." I place a soft kiss on his lips before walking away.

Is it obvious my words aren't matching how I'm feeling? Tonight, everything shifted. After my mother died, my father withdrew from any public life and made sure I was always shielded from the life we once had. Tonight, reminded me what life in the public eye means and I'm not sure it's the life I want to live.

Slipping into the white two-piece, I give myself a once over in the mirror. I mean, this life isn't so bad. Traveling to exotic places, dinner at fancy restaurants, shopping with no budget. These are all things a girl could get very used to.

"We'll meet you guys out there. I'm gonna go see what's taking Johana so long." I hear Bennett from down the hall. The distinct slap of his flip flops gets louder as he approaches our room.

Bennett closes the door behind him; his eyes grow wide as he scans every inch of my body.

"Damn." His voice is practically a growl as he stalks towards me. Bennett's hands begin at my shoulders and glide down to my ass, running his fingers on the inside of the bathing suit bottoms. "I don't know why we even bought you this thing, when all I can think about is getting you out of it."

"Because teasing you is half the fun." I run my finger down his perfectly sculpted abs.

"Sweet lips, I'm so sorry about tonight. If it takes a thousand lifetimes, I will make it up to you."

"First, that sounded like a cheesy soap opera line. And second, I told you to stop. Yes, I was mad at first, but then I remembered something my mom once told me. Once you step in front of the camera, you are always in the public eye. When I was a little girl, I walked into my mother's bedroom to find her in tears. She said people in the magazines were saying mean things about her. I remember telling her in my five-year-old little brave voice to never let bullies dull your sparkle."

"The tabloids can be evil," he says.

"Years later, I found the article and strangely enough I remember the night like it was yesterday because it was the dinner party we had for my grandmother's one-hundredth birthday. I remember my parents having an argument in the car about not letting my mother's celebrity status interfere with my grandmother's celebration. Later that evening, people were asking for pictures and autographs and my mother kept politely turning them down. A week later, she was in every tabloid as Hollywood's newest bitch. After that, she never said no again. I can't even imagine what it's like now in the time of social media."

"It's a fine line between wanting a private life and becoming the next hashtag joke. Still doesn't mean it's okay to leave you alone at a restaurant for almost an hour."

"I guess I'll just have to find something else for you to eat later," I tease.

"Oh, sweet lips, I'm starving for you right now."

"Too bad you told our friends we'd met them out there." I shrug, grab the ties on his board shorts and pull him behind me.

Chapter Eighteen

Adam

I'm mere inches from one of the most beautiful women I have ever met, and yet I still can't take my eyes off Joey. The white two-piece, hugs each of her curves in places I no longer want to resist.

Bennett pours her a glass of champagne; they link arms before taking a drink. Makes me sick. It was only an hour ago she was on the phone with me at dinner because Mr. Wonderful ditched her for a stranger's wedding.

"I think it would hurt, don't you?" Bree asks, breaking me from distraction.

"Huh? Oh yeah, it would hurt."

"Are you even listening to me?"

"Oh, Bree, honey, get used to it. He's got the ability to tune someone out at the drop of a hat. You could be looking directly at him and he won't hear a thing you say," Joey chimes in.

She slinks down into the hot tub, sitting directly across from me.

"Most guys are like that." Bennett comes to my defense, taking the seat next to her. "What were you guys talking about?"

"A couple of the frat and sorority houses at my school are doing this playground games competition for charity. One of the girls in my sociology class asked me to be on their team."

"Sounds like fun," he says. "What kind of games are we talking about here?"

"Tug-of-war, red rover, dodgeball, beer pong, and truth or dare."

"I fucking love truth or dare," blurts Johana. "Adam, do you remember the last time we played? Oh my god, it was hysterical. We were, like, fourteen and daring people do shit, like jump in a pool with their clothes on or go eat something totally disgusting."

"We should play adult truth or dare!" Bree suggests, wiggling her eyebrows.

"Hell, yes we should!" Joey downs her glass of champagne and raises her glass for another.

With a snap of a finger, Bennett has the bartenders refilling our glasses.

"Are you sure this is a good idea?" I ask.

"Stop being such a fuddy-duddy and have some fun. I mean, isn't the point of this whole vacation to get to know each other? How better than a friendly little game of truth or dare." Joey's devious smirk, calling my chicken with her eyes, has always been my kryptonite. I can't say no to her.

"I'll start," Bree begins. "Bennett, truth or dare?"

"Let's start off with a bang and go with a dare."

"Hand me your phone," she says.

A confused Bennett unlocks his phone, handing it to her. She scrolls through his contacts, eyes growing wide. "You know a lot of famous people, but as I spy the number of Jaxon Molina, the hottest of all the superhero actors, I know the perfect dare. Bennett, I dare you to call Jaxon Molina and ask if the rumors about him having a guiche piercing are true?"

"Seriously? I've only met him once. I barely know the guy."

"Yup! You wanted to play. Tell him you're looking for advice to spice things up for the new lady."

Shit. Bree is vicious. Man to man, you don't ask another guy about his junk piercings. Not wanting to back down from a dare, Bennett pushes send.

"Voicemail," he says, with a sigh of relief.

"Leave a message. A dare's a dare."

"Shit. Okay. Um… Hey, Jaxon. My girlfriend and her friend here are just curious if the rumor about your dick piercing is true. Yeah, um, okay. Bye." Bennett's head shakes in embarrassment as he ends the call.

"My turn! My turn!" Joey's amusement in playing this game is entertaining. "Okay, bestie Adam. Truth or dare?"

"I'm gonna go with truth after watching Bennett's face turn fifty shades of red."

"Boring," Joey teases.

I shrug and roll my eyes.

"Mind if I ask the question?" Bree intervenes.

"Not at all." Joey smiles from ear to ear, finishing another glass of champagne.

"If Johana wasn't dating Bennett, would you be here with her instead of me?"

"Seriously? We're going there again? Joey and I are friends. That's all. And she *is* with Bennett and I *am* with you. So, the question is moot."

"So, kiss her," Bree instructs.

"What?" This chick must be off her fucking rocker. Joey or Bennett will surely put a stop to this, right?

"Since you actually didn't answer your truth question, I dare you to kiss Johana."

Fuck it. This is the moment I stop being a pussy and man up. I stand, taking just two steps to reach her. I lift her up, so we are standing face to face. "A dare is a dare, right?"

Not wanting to overstep, my lips gently brush hers. Joey's arms reach around my neck, bringing our bodies closer than our lips. With a soft moan, her mouth opens and her tongue is exploring mine. Being the gentleman I am, it's only right of me to return her kiss.

Joey's knees buckle. Catching her, I break our connection, whispering "I got you" in her ear only loud enough for the two of us to hear.

I slide back to my seat, praying the bubbles from the jets will hide my raging hard-on.

I would trade never having sex with another woman again for another first kiss with Johana.

"See. Nothing. Nada. Skidding out in the friend zone." She's buying my sack of shit. "Okay, babe. Truth or dare?"

"I'm going to follow Bennett's sense of adventure and go with dare."

"Oh, oh, oh," drunk Joey chimes in. "I got a good one. I dare you to choose one person here and do your best fake orgasm while looking them directly in the eyes.

"Since you and Adam got to have all the fun with the last dare, it's only fair Bennett and I have a little of our own."

Breeann straddles Bennett's lap and their eyes lock. Using his shoulders for leverage, she moves her body back and forth, grinding herself against him.

"Oh fuck. Oh yes. Right there. Fuck, you feel so good." Bree's sultry voice is made for the dirtiest of words. Her excitement builds with each intense moan escaping her body. "Deeper, baby. Fuck. Fuck. Fuck. So close, don't stop. Don't. Stop." Her movements slow. She moves her face closer to his, deepening the eye contact. "You ready? It's so much hotter when two people orgasm together."

Bennett nods, eyes wide and locked on Bree's. "Fuck, I'm ready. I need to come. Fuck! Fuck! Fuck!"

She rides harder and faster with every orgasmic scream she releases.

When Joey dared Bree to fake an orgasm, I don't think she planned for the dry hump realism she's getting. Her chest heaves with excitement.

"All right, Bennett, your turn," Bree says, climbing off his lap.

He turns to Joey. "Sweet lips, truth or dare?"

"Truth. Definitely, truth." She drunk giggles with her answer.

"When did you lose your virginity?"

I'm just as curious about her answer. The night Joey told me she had already lost her virginity, I was devastated. I had always thought it would be her and I and when it wasn't, I never asked any more questions.

"Easy. Freshman year of college, Mario De Luca, in the backseat of his brand-new Audi." Her eyes dart to mine, then quickly away as she realizes what she just admitted. Joey quickly downs another glass of champagne. "The story is nothing exciting. It's not worth telling."

"Nope. You have to give us the whole truth. Your game. Your rules," I remind her. "If you don't tell us, we'll have to give you one of those fun dares to do."

"It wasn't what I envisioned. He was the president of the frat linked to my sorority house. And a senior. I had been crushing on him for a while. We had been hanging out all night at the annual Monster Mash party. Since I was only eighteen and one of the few who hadn't been drinking, he asked me to drive him to the store. One thing led to another and we ended up driving out to the beach and I lost my virginity in the backseat of his car. I thought we'd date at least until he graduated, but we never spoke again."

An instant heat rushes through my body and my blood is reaching a boiling point. This is caused by the increased temperature but the anger of being lied to for the past decade.

"Mario De Luca?" Bennett questions. "Would his father happen to be Dante De Luca, the director?"

"It is. Please don't tell me you know him," Johana begs.

"Dante, yes. He actually directed the last movie I worked on. Mario,was in Canada visiting and had to be physically escorted off set for harassing the women."

"You sure do know how to pick 'em." Words intended for my head come busting out of my lips much louder than expected.

"What was that?" Bennett questions my comment.

"Nothing. I'm gonna call it a night. My head's spinning. This whole concussion thing and all."

"Want me to come with you?" Bree asks.

"Nope. Stay. Enjoy yourself. I will see you all in the morning."

As I'm packing and taking my ass home.

"A penny for your thoughts," Joey says, joining me on the sand early the next morning to watch the early morning surfers.

"You wouldn't want to hear my thoughts for all the money in the world."

Last night, Joey broke my heart in a way I believe she completely understands.

The virginity pact was her idea. Then she lied.

"I'm sorry."

"This is way beyond sorry, Johana. You should have just been honest with me. Was the thought of having sex with me so awful to you?"

"Not awful, Adam. Terrifying. The thought was terrifying. You're my best friend. It was a silly pact made by a heartbroken sixteen-year-old. Look at what happened to Mario and me. What if that was us?"

My eyes meet hers for the first time since she sat next to me. Their bright blue shine has faded to a sad, foggy gray, surrounded by a red puffiness telling me she's been crying for hours. It doesn't stop me from shooting daggers right back at her.

"You're comparing me to some frat guy you fucked in the back of a car? Seriously?"

"Sex changes people. I saw it with Royce after she started sleeping with every guy she dated. I thought if we slept together, right before we both went off to college, it would change everything between us. You were the most important person in my life. I couldn't risk losing you."

"I'm not upset because you slept with someone else. I'm hurt because you chose to lie to me. The one thing we promised we'd never do. Then you kept it from me for ten years. And if it wasn't for a drunken game of truth or dare, I may have never known you're capable of such deceit." I stand to leave before Joey can see the tears welling up.

"Adam."

"I booked a flight home. Bree and I are leaving this evening. I just can't do this anymore, Johana."

"Do what, Adam? Kauai? Us? What are you talking about?" Her voice cracks as she starts to cry.

"Yes." I walk away, leaving her sitting on the shore.

With sixteen years of friendship, Joey and I have had our fair share of fights, but for the first time, I feel like this can actually come between us. I was seriously naive enough to believe Joey and I didn't keep secrets from one another.

"I can't believe your work called you back." Bree pouts as she packs her bags. It was the only lie that wouldn't cause any more heartbreak for anyone. "I mean, tonight is the luau with Richard Grovanski. You couldn't have told the hospital there were no flights until tomorrow."

"I told you to stay if you want, but I need to get back. The hospital needs me," I say coldly, leaving no room for discussion.

"This trip was a mistake in the first place," I grumble under my breath.

"Does this have something to do with the game of truth or dare we played last night? Your entire demeanor changed after Johana told the story about losing her virginity."

"Don't be ridiculous. I got a text from work. That's that. You want to see it?" I pray she says no.

"Sorry. Call it a woman's intuition. You're hiding something."

"Whatever. Finish packing, say your goodbyes, and I'll meet you in the car."

I grab the packed bags, high-tailing my way through the living room, not wanting to talk to anyone. This trip has ripped my world apart and I'm ready to escape this paradise turned hell.

"So, you're really going to leave without saying goodbye?" Joey surprises me from around the corner.

"That was the plan."

"Adam," she pleads. "You have to understand why I didn't tell you. I thought I was protecting us."

"How ironic, because you may have destroyed us for good. You just don't get it. I don't think you'll ever get it."

~

I take a deep breath of the crisp morning mountain air. The mix of fresh pine and piping hot coffee awakens each sense of my body. The hospital covered my shifts, and the last thing I wanted to do was drift around in my apartment alone, so I decided to head up to Big Bear. My family bought a cabin up here in the nineties. Now we mainly use it when we want to escape the craziness of L.A.

"A penny for your thoughts?" A female voice startles me from behind.

"Ugh. What is with that stupid saying? My thoughts are worth way more than a penny."

"Ew. What crawled up your ass and died, big brother?" Coincidently, Mandi needed an escape this weekend as well.

The *Bettie Wites* dropped a new album this week and the next few days are filled with press junkets and parties—not the best place for a woman who's seven months pregnant.

"Sorry. Just dealing with some shit. You wouldn't understand."

"Try me. I'm young, but I'm smart."

"And you've also been in love with the same person since you were eight."

"So, is this about Bree or Johana?" she asks. Despite the six-year age difference, my sister and I have always been close. She seems to understand me better than anyone else in my life.

"All of the above," I say, slightly defeated.

For the next hour, I let it all out. Everything about Bree, Hawaii, Bennett, and especially Joey. Mandi just listens, never questioning, or thinking I'm overreacting. She just listens, which is a bit frustrating.

"Say something."

"What do you want me to say? There's nothing I can say that you don't already know. You've been in love with Johana for just as long as I've loved Lincoln. Only difference is, neither one of you have been able to man up and admit it. I don't understand what you two are afraid of because being with your other half is the greatest feeling in the world."

"Maybe Bennett is Joey's other half."

Her nose scrunches with a confused look. "Whatcha talkin' 'bout, Willis?"

"What? Who the hell is Willis?"

"Sorry. Linc and I have been watching reruns of this old 80s tv show and it's the kid's catch phrase. In all seriousness, you know as well as I do Bennett Blakely is not Johana's other half. She's not cut out to be the celebrity wife."

"What do I do? If I tell her how I feel and she chooses Bennett, our friendship is over. Or, what if we try and then crash and burn?"

"'Tis better to have loved and lost than to never have loved at all."

"You're just full of fun little quotes this morning, aren't you?"

Mandi giggles, her face glowing on the verge of motherhood. "All I'm saying is go for it. Trust your gut, Adam. I did, and look where it got me." She rubs her growing belly.

"Yeah, I don't want to be pregnant," I tease.

"You're such an idiot." Her bony little elbow jabs my ribs, just like when we were kids.

Wrapping my arm around my sister's shoulders, I pull her close to me. "I try. Thanks for listening. Now I just need to figure out what to do."

"Jump, big brother. The landing will be worth the fall."

Chapter Nineteen

Johana

It's been almost two weeks since I've seen or heard from Adam. Only once in our friendship, have we ever gone this long without talking. It's killing me to know he's no longer just a phone call away.

Sitting on the patio stairs, I'm mesmerized by the stillness of the ocean this morning. Some mornings the water looks like glass, still, with nothing able to disrupt its serenity. Then out of nowhere, a storm kicks up, sending chaos throughout one's world.

"Wanna talk about it?" Bella joins me, handing me a hot cup of coffee.

"He's never going to talk to me again, is he?"

"Let me break it down to you, princess," she teases with her horrible New York accent, trying to get me to crack a smile. It didn't work. "Maybe. Maybe not. I've been saying for years that boy is head over heels in love with you and has been since the day you met. I'm not sure if you are seriously blind or just too stubborn to not see it. Adam has stood by you through thick and thin almost your entire life. But between Bennett and this lie, he may have hit his breaking point."

"We kissed."

"Who? You and Adam? When? Why am I just now hearing about this?"

"During the game of truth or dare. Bree said if there was nothing between us then we should kiss."

"And?" Bella presses.

"It was okay, I guess." Who am I kidding? It was one of the greatest kisses of my life. Heat rushed through my body like a wildfire. My heart raced like it was in a marathon. Thank God we were in a jacuzzi or someone may have seen how wet I in fact was.

"You're lying. It's too cold out here for your cheeks to be that red already."

"It was really hot. Like, I'm Bennett 'fricken' Blakely's girlfriend. One of the hottest men on the planet chose me and all I can think about is Adam's tongue caressing mine. He tasted like champagne with a hint of salt water. It was like nothing I ever experienced before or am sure I want to again."

"You definitely want to because if you didn't you would be sitting here gushing all about it." Bella's right. She's always right and she knows it. I did like kissing Adam. Part of me wants to kiss him again to prove the way I'm feeling is from that first kiss flutter. The smarter part of me knows those who play with fire only get burned.

"Only three days left until the end of month and true love has yet to make a surprise visit. I told you the psychic we went to in San Francisco was a bunch of hocus pocus," I complain to Bella as I flip through the latest issue of Cosmo magazine.

"Today, we finished our last finals of the year and officially became seniors. I plan on hitting up every party at every frat house I can find. Maybe when you see one of the guys at the Kappa house doing the keg stands they are so famous for, true love will smack you in the face."

"Ew. Not in this lifetime." I throw a small pillow from my bed, hitting her upside the head.

"Johana, you have a visitor," one of my sorority sisters yells from the bottom of the stairs.

"Seriously, if you sent me a stripper, I'm gonna kick your ass," I joke, glaring at my roommate.

"No, but thanks for the idea, because I will definitely use that sometime in the future."

Just as curious as I am, Bella follows me downstairs. I haven't a clue who would be visiting me. I've been single for the better part of the year, as far as I know my father is still on honeymoon number five, and all my friends live in my sorority house with me.

All of my friends, except…

"Adam? What are you doing here? Why aren't you in L.A. taking finals?" I throw my arms around his neck, hugging my best friend tight. I'm happy to see him, no matter what the reason.

"Ah ha! I knew it!" Bella chimes in from the stairwell.

"Shut it." I glare at my friend, sending daggers with my eyes if I could. My friend dramatically pretends to be hit and she makes her way back upstairs to our room.

"I finished them up early. Something I should know?" Adam asks, raising an eyebrow in suspicion.

"Nope." I nonchalantly shake my head. "Hungry? Let me grab my purse. We'll go grab a burger and beer."

I take the stairs two at a time, slamming my door behind me. "What the hell is Adam doing here?" I ask Bella like she's supposed to know.

"Maybe the psychic wasn't wrong after all." She smirks as I leave the room.

Walking into Antonio's Nut House, I'm greeted by name, from all three bartenders.

"Come here a lot?" Adam asks.

"Occasionally." I giggle. We take the only table left in the back corner.

"Joester!" The waiter bounces onto the seat next to me. "How dare you bring in this hot piece of arm candy and not bring his even hotter gay brother for me. Please tell me there's a gay brother." He looks at Adam, batting his long eyelashes.

"Adam, this is Chad, my overly eager-"

"And horny," he chimes in.

"And horny, new gay best friend. Chad, this is Adam, from back home."

"The Adam? I feel like I already know ya, man. Heard a lot about you."

Adam squints in confusion. "Sorry, can't say the same."

"Yeah, that's usually how it goes. The usual, babe?" Chad asks.

"Make it two."

"So, what's going on?" I start to press Adam. I know my best friend better than I know myself. Adam is not the spontaneous, five-hour solo road trip type. He's more of what'd you call the preplanner boy scout type.

"What can't a guy just come visit his best friend for the weekend? You've always said, I can come visit anytime."

"Adam? Did something happen between you and Heidi? Did something happen at school?"

"It's been a long day. Can we just relax and we'll talk in the morning?"

"I hate that idea, but I know your 'can we' just means we'll talk tomorrow."

"You know me so well. Now, let's shoot some pool before your usual comes."

Adam holds his hand out and leads me to the billiards table. Adam's family had a table in their game room growing up. The hours we spent playing high school have made me quite a little hustler in the bar.

"Careful," the guy at the next table warns Adam. "One night, she took me for a hundred and fifty bucks. She looks cute but she's got a bite."

"Don't be bitter. I gave you the chance to win it back double or nothing. You quit."

"Are you making that much playing pool?" he asks.

"Just enough to pay my tab here."

"Which isn't cheap," Chad chimes in, setting the tequila shots and beers down on the table.

"Neither are our shopping trips each month," I tease.

"Touché, honey." He pretends to zip his lips and skips back to the bar.

"What has gotten into you?" Adam asks.

"Good evening, Nut House! Who's ready to rock with us tonight? We are the Bastard Spiders. Enjoy."

With each tequila shot down, Adam and I dance a little closer. I grind a little harder each time he slips his hand around my waist. When the bulge in his pants presses against my ass, I know I have the same effect on him I always have. Moving with the beat of the music our bodies grow closer than they've ever been. Right now, I want Adam more than I've ever wanted any man before.

I lean back and whisper, "Ready to get out of here?"

"You ready to go home?"

"I'm ready to go wherever you're staying." He pulls out his phone and calls us an Uber. "Five minutes."

Stumbling into the hotel room, we fall on the bed laughing. "I'm glad you're here, Adam. I didn't realize how much I've needed you." We lay on the bed facing each other; our fingers intertwine.

What if the psychic was right? Adam was an unexpected visit. He could be my true love. I regret not letting Adam be my first time, but I was scared. But now I know what I'm doing. I'm confident in my body and my womanhood. I know now I wouldn't disappoint him. Hell, I may even impress him.

His loud snore interrupts the ramblings in my head. Adam has passed out.

I wake in the morning to an empty bed. Adam is on the patio, talking to someone on the phone. My eyes lock on his strong back and broad shoulders; I bite my lip thinking about Adam's arms pinning me down while sucking on my hard nipples.

I should not be thinking this way about Adam. Yet, I can't stop and I don't think I want to. This could go really good or really bad.

"Hey, sleepy head. You're finally awake."

"Fuck you. It's not even eight in the morning. Who was on the phone?"

"Heidi. I haven't talked to her since I left."

"You left her?"

"No, left to visit up here."

"Oh. Why are you here, Adam?"

"So, yeah. I wanted to tell you in person," he stammers. "Heidi wants to take our relationship to the next level. We're moving in together."

"Is moving in with her what you want?"

"I think so. It seems like the logical step after a year of dating, right?"

"Why are you asking me? I can't get a guy to stick around more than a couple months."

"I'm asking you because you're my voice of reason. You're the person who's not afraid to kick me in the ass when I'm about to make a royal mistake."

Big sign from the universe right there. If Adam were my true love, he definitely wouldn't be making plans to move in with another woman. Just proves me right about the psychic being a bunch of phony bologna.

"You need to do whatever makes you happy, Adam."

Pulling my car into the parking spot reserved for Bennett Blakely, my heart races. I take a deep breath to calm myself. Why am I nervous? I've met Bennett on the set before, but this is the first time since I began questioning my relationship with Adam.

"Hi, sweet lips," Bennett opens my door, greeting me.

"Hey." My voice is shaky. He helps me out of the car, bringing my body close to his, kissing me like he can't get enough. The nerves instantly leave my body. I remind myself how lucky I am to be the girlfriend of one of the sexiest men alive.

This afternoon is Mandi and Lincoln's baby shower. Bennett had a few scenes to finish filming and suggested I pick him up on set.

"I have one more scene the director wants to reshoot and then I'm all yours for the rest of the weekend."

"No problem. I'll just wait in the car."

"I want you to come watch. Sheridan is shooting the man who killed my twin sister. It's pretty intense."

"Wait. I've been watching Hope's Landing since before I can remember. You don't have a twin sister."

"What a plot twist, right? Come on."

Linking our hands together, Bennett leads me inside. I feel like a kid walking into Disneyland for the first time. Hope Memorial Hospital to my right, Hope's Landing City Square to my left. It's like walking into another world.

"Where are you filming today?" I ask.

"Out back, at the docks." Bennett directs me to his personalized director's chair, kisses my forehead before taking his place on set.

"Let's try and make this our last take, people. My girl and I have places to be." Bennett looks over at me and smiles.

"Jack, when Emily shoots you, make the fall look more realistic. Stop overacting. And action!"

Being that soap operas are filmed six months in advance, I have no idea what's going on but I'm completely enthralled. Watching your favorite television show in real life is a bit surreal.

Chills run through my spine when the other actor takes out a gun and points it at Bennett.

"I don't have a twin sister. The orphanage I was adopted from told my parents I was an only child."

"They thought you were. Your father was a despicable man. Our mother died while giving birth to you and your sister. He didn't want the two of you and he definitely didn't want her bastard child. So, he dumped all three of us at different orphanages, claiming we are all only children. He never wanted us to make a connection to each other or back to him."

"So why did you kill our sister?" Bennett asks in his characters, deep southern accent, I find incredibly attractive.

"The moment you two were born my life was ruined. Everything was taken from me. Now I will take everything from you."

As he's about to pull the trigger, Sheridan, Bennett's onscreen fiancé, comes in from behind, firing one single shot killing the evil half-brother. Bennett spins around, and without a single word, the two embrace in a passionate soap opera kiss.

The chills in my spine turn to an uncomfortable jealousy. I understand kissing other women is just part of his job. When I watch it on television, I'm able to separate fiction from reality; seeing it in person is a whole other ball game. I wish Bennett would have warned me.

"Cut! Excellent. Perfect. Wonderful adlib kiss at the end there, Emily. Alright everybody, have a great weekend," the director shouts.

Bennett waves me over to him on set. "I wanted you two to meet. Johana, this is Emily Buchman, who you know plays my fiancé, Sheridan, on the show. Emily, this is my girlfriend, Johana Warner."

"I finally get to meet the girlfriend this one can't stop talking about." Rather than reaching for my hand, she awkwardly puts her arm around Bennett's waist.

"It's a pleasure to meet you. I've been watching *Hope's Landing* for over twenty years."

"That's almost longer than I've been alive." Emily chuckles in a way that makes my skin crawl. I can instantly tell this is a girl I do not like.

"Are you ready to go, baby? If we don't hit the road soon, we'll hit nothing but traffic on our way to Santa Barbara for the weekend." Bennett holds his hand out for mine, completely oblivious to Emily's rude comment.

The car ride has been virtually silent since we left the studio. For one of the first times in my life, I'm at a loss for words.

"What's swirling in that pretty little head of yours, sweet lips?"

To my left, is one of the most gorgeous men on the planet. He makes his living off being a steamy soap actor. I should be lucky he chose me but watching him kiss other women is not something I want to do again.

"The kiss seemed so real. It was uncomfortable to watch."

"You watch the show. You've seen me kiss Emily hundreds of times."

"I've watched Ryan Hope kiss Sheridan Fitzgerald on television. It's different than watching Bennett Blakely kiss Emily Buchman in person."

"I'm sorry, Johana. The last thing I'd wanna do is make you feel uncomfortable. I had no idea Emily was planning on adding a kiss at the end of the scene."

"That's what worries me," I admit.

Stopped in traffic, he takes my chin in his strong hand and brushes his thumb against my bottom lip. "These are the only lips I ever think about. You have nothing to worry about, baby. Johana, I love you. I know we haven't said it yet and this isn't the romantic setting I wanted, but I feel like it's the perfect time to tell you."

"You… You love me?" It's been a long time since someone has said those words to me and I feel like they truly mean it.

"I do. Don't act so shocked. There is so much to be loved about you and I want to be the man to do it. I understand if you're not ready to say it back and that's okay. I just wanted you to know where I'm at."

As our fingers intertwine, I lean my head against his shoulder and smile. Bennett leans down kissing my forehead. His kisses make me feel warm and protected.

I'm glad Bennett decided to join me this weekend. We'll get through this shower, and then spend the rest of the weekend curled up in a beachside villa, figuring each other out.

I'm just glad Adam had to work. I couldn't handle him and Bennett in the same weekend.

Chapter Twenty

Adam

Being honest about my feelings is something which has never come easily to me. It's the reason I avoid most intimate relationships. That and the fact I've been in love with the same girl since I was twelve years old.

My feelings for Joey are not fair to Bree. As much as I hate to hurt her, lying to her is much worse. Back in high school, I would have just done something stupid to make the girl break-up with me. Life was so much easier back then.

"Sorry, I'm late. The photographer was super picky about every move I made." Bree kisses my cheek and takes the seat next to me. We made plans over a week ago to meet at Duke's in Huntington Beach after a modeling shoot she had on the pier.

"No problem." I can't make eye contact with her. I feel like such a coward.

"Adam, what's wrong? You looked like someone just kicked your dog."

"We gotta talk," I mumble, nervously. Maybe I shouldn't have chosen to do this in a public place but I was afraid if we were at home I would cave to her tears.

"You're scaring me. What's going on?"

"I care about you, Bree. I really do, but I'm-"

"In love with Johana," she interrupts. "I know. I've always known. I was just hoping I might be the one to break down the walls you've put up."

"I'm sorry. I never meant to lead you on. I've been in love with her since the day we met. She's my penguin."

"It's okay. I felt like I always knew this day would come. After watching you kiss her, I knew I didn't have a chance in hell in holding your heart. Have you talked to Johana about this yet?"

"No. I've tried over the years, but it never comes out right."

"You better man up and tell her. If Bennett beats you to the punch, you may never get another chance. He's her fantasy but you're her knight in shining armor. You need to swoop in on your white horse before the princess runs off with the handsome prince."

"Thank you for understanding. Again, I'm sorry. I never meant to hurt you."

Bree shrugs. "It was fun while it lasted. And I got a free trip to Hawaii out of it, so I can't complain too much. And you're still buying me dinner. I'm starving."

Whoever thought up the idea of co-ed baby showers must have been off their rocker. Men don't want to be at these things. We could care less how many onesies you get or who can guess the mystery flavor of baby food. But somehow my sister convinced her boyfriend and all his rockstar friends to show up at this thing.

Standing in the kitchen, helping my mom prepare the food, the collective gasp could be heard from two rooms away. Followed by a roomful of whispers and schoolgirl giggles.

"Johana! Bennett! I'm so glad you're here," Mandi says purposely loud enough for me to hear.

"You and Mandi both reassured me she wasn't coming." I scowl at my mother.

"We lied," she says, nonchalantly shrugging her shoulders. "Mandi told me about your conversation in Big Bear. Plus, I know how miserable you've been not talking to her."

"You and my sister need to mind your own business. I'll talk to Joey when I'm ready. A baby shower is not the time or place."

Hearing footsteps approaching the kitchen, I duck into the fridge, pretending to look for something as a lame excuse to hide.

"Annie!" Joey hugs my mom as usual. "Thanks so much for having us."

"Of course, Johana. You know you are like a daughter to me. And technically you are my grandchild's step-aunt removed by divorce."

"That's a bit of a stretch, but I'll take it. Is something wrong with that person? He's had his head in the fridge for a while," Joey whispers to my mom.

Feeling like a total idiot, I stand up, turn around and face the music. "Hey."

"Um, I thought you had to work?"

"And I was told you weren't coming, but here we are." I grab a beer and head out back with the other men to avoid the drama. I know I need to talk to Joey, but I don't know what I want to say. Because honestly, I don't know how much more I can take.

Before I have a chance to finish my first beer, Bennett sits down, handing me another. "What's up between you and Johana?" he bluntly asks.

"I don't know what you're talking about." I try to play dumb, but Bennett isn't stupid.

"C'mon, man. Have you guys even talked since you left Kauai? Did you guys have some kind of fight?"

"I've been busy." I take a long swig off my beer, trying to avoid any further conversation.

"I told Johana I loved her on the way up here today," Bennett shares with me like we're old friends.

"I'm sure you two will be very happy together. Excuse me." I abruptly leave, not waiting to hear what her response was.

Retreating to the solitude of my parents' bedroom, the quiet gives me time to breathe.

"I needed this weekend to be Joey free. I just need to figure this shit out," I say out loud, talking to myself.

"Seriously? A Joey-free weekend? You haven't spoken to me in two weeks." Joey scares the shit out of me, coming out of my parents' private bathroom door.

"What the ever-loving fuck? Are you stalking me?"

"Your mom said I could use her bathroom for more privacy. And you're the one outside my bathroom door. Maybe you're stalking me. What do you need to figure out?" she asks.

Damn, I was hoping she didn't hear me. "Nothing. Don't worry about it. All you need to think about is how much you and Bennett are in love."

Her brow scrunches in confusion.

"Bennett told me. Congratulations. It's been a long time since you've been in love. Ian, right?"

I'm not sure why I feel the need to be so spiteful. Maybe it's jealousy. Maybe it's a broken heart. Maybe I just want her to hurt the way I'm hurting.

Mandi startles us both as she comes busting through the door. "Good. You two have finally made up. Now, come on, Linc and I are about to open presents. When Tallulah Violet looks back on her baby shower video, I want her to see Uncle Adam and Aunt Johana have been there since the very beginning."

We are ushered out before we can even begin to argue.

Thirty minutes into diapers, onesies, and anything and everything pink and gray, I lose all interest. I slither my way through the hundred strangers gathered in my parents' living room, successfully going unnoticed. I'm rewarded with an empty patio and full cooler.

No sooner do I put the beer to my lips, when I hear the patio doors shut behind me.

"Mind if I join you?" Bennett asks.

Peaceful escape, ruined.

"Baby showers not your thing either?

"Not at all," I answer. "I'm excited for my sister and can't wait to do this one day with my future wife. There's just some things on my mind today."

"We're a different breed, man."

"How so?" I ask.

"Baby showers, kids, families, it's not for me. I'm a Hollywood workaholic. I love acting and all the thrills and perks that come with it. I'm not willing to give my life up for kids. I'd rather travel than change diapers."

"Have you told Joey this?"

"Nah. If she can't even say *I love you* back to me, we're not ready to have the kid talk."

Wait. What the hell? Joey didn't say it back to him? Could I possibly still have a chance?

I think it's time to put "Plan Capture my Penguin" into action.

"Hey," I say.

"Hey."

"I'm sorry," we say in unison.

I pull Joey into a long hug before we both take the seats across from each other at our favorite bar, the Beach Ball, right on the beach in Newport. For the first time ever, there's an awkward silence between us, neither of us knowing where to begin.

"I should have never lied to you, Adam. For as long as I've known you, we've always been a hundred percent honest with each other. I was so afraid sex would ruin us. Besides my mother, you're the only person in the world who truly understands me, who loves me, flaws, and all. Do you know how many of our friends slept together in high school and then hated each other soon after? I needed you too much to let that happen. I still need you."

"I get it. I'm still hurt that you kept it from me for so long and the fact you lost your virginity in the back seat of some guy's car. The one place you always swore you'd never have sex." I have to make light of the situation if we are going to move forward.

"It's actually kind of fun," she jokes. Note to self- car sex with Joey is an option.

"Well, I'm sorry for acting like such a jerk. I was hurt and angry. And honestly, heartbroken you kept this secret from me."

"Will you ever forgive me? How can I ever make it up to you?" She bats her long beautiful eyelashes at me.

Oh, beautiful, you have no idea how bad I want to answer your question with so many inappropriate things. "How 'bout we start with another round of drinks here."

"Perfect. Charles, another round here, please," Joey shouts to the bartender. "And keep 'em coming."

Four rounds and two hours later, we walk along the shore, toes tickled by the water, watching the sunset paint the sky with brilliant shades of pinks and purples. Joey stops along the way to pet every dog she sees.

"Do you love him?" I'm just drunk enough to have the courage to ask.

"The German Shepherd that just tried to make out with me? I mean, he's cute and all, but not my type," she jokes, purposefully deflecting the question.

Not letting her, I continue my inquiry. "In Kauai, you asked what I thought about Bennett because you were ready to tell him you loved him. Why didn't you say it back to him?"

"How do you know about that?"

"He said something to me about it at the baby shower." I stand in front of her, staring deeply in the blue eyes I live to get lost in. "A month ago, you were ready to say it. When Bennett told you, he loves you didn't say it back. What changed?"

Johana's eyes immediately shift to her toes shuffling in the sand between us. I gently lift her chin, forcing her to keep eye contact. "No secrets," I whisper.

"Our kiss."

Without a second thought of the consequences, my mouth crashes against hers. My tongue moves with hers sending shockwaves through every inch of my body. Needing more, I wrap my arms around her waist pulling her closer to me.

Johana throws her hands to my chest, pushing me back and breaking our connection. "I… I gotta go."

She's out of my arms before I have half a chance to stop her. "Joey, stop," I shout. She waves me off without even turning around. "Joey, please stop." I start to chase after her.

"Thanks for the drinks. I'll call you tomorrow." She disappears over the berm. Did I just royally fuck everything up?

Waking up the next morning, my head is pounding from the overabundance of whiskey I consumed last night. My room is dark, except for the flashing blue light on my cell. Hopefully, the universe called to tell me last night was just a bad dream.

No such luck. It's a text from Bella.

Bella: *What time do you work today? We need to talk.*

Me: 3pm. *What's up? Is Joey okay?*

Bella: *I'll be by in 30 minutes.*

Me: *Okay. Bring coffee.*

If Bella wants to talk, I'm either gaining an ally or an enemy. There's no doubt she's heard about the kisses Joey and I have now shared. Bella has seen through me since day one and has always loved giving me shit about it. I'm not sure how she feels about Joey's relationship with Bennett.

"Hey! Nurse Nutsack. Open up." Isabella knocks exactly thirty minutes later.

"Tits McGee. To what do I owe the pleasure of your visit?"

"We need to talk," she says, pushing her way past me and into my living room.

"Is Joey okay?" I ask again.

"I don't know. You tell me. She said she was meeting up with you and then came home drunk and in tears."

"We kissed," I admit.

"Again?" Okay, so she knew about Kauai, but not about last night. "You two need to figure your shit out."

"Is she happy with Bennett?"

"She is. But he's not who Johana's meant to be with."

"And you know this how?" I question.

"Do you remember when you came to visit after junior year to tell Johana about moving in with Heidi?"

"Biggest mistake of my life, but yeah I remember the trip."

"Earlier in the month, Johana and I visited a psychic. She was skeptical but went along for the fun of it. The psychic told Jo her true love would make a surprise visit before the end of the month. Nothing happens all month. Then lo and behold, three days before the month is over, you show up. Did you know she wanted to sleep with you that night? But your dumb ass passed out and got up the next morning to tell her you were moving in with your girlfriend. She closed her heart to love for a long time after that."

"I had no idea."

"You need to step up, Adam. I don't know how many chances you'll get before you lose her for good."

"If I haven't already. Why would Johana choose me when Bennett could offer her everything she's dreamed of?"

"Not everything," she says.

"Please tell me what I have. I'd love to hear it," I snap back.

Bella places her hand on my chest, directly over my heart and pats twice. "Think about it. Johana has her own money. She doesn't need Bennett's. Sure, his perks are fun, but you know damn well none of that means anything to her. All she's ever wanted is someone to give her life she never had."

"How do I convince Joey to trust me with heart? Everything I've tried for the past sixteen years has been a massive failure."

"I think I have a few tricks up my sleeve. Keep your phone close. I'll text you soon."

She jumps up and takes off without saying anything else. I hope Bella knows what she's doing. This is my last shot and I need to make it work.

Chapter Twenty-One

Johana

I've spent the last two days locked in the solitude of my bedroom. I haven't answered my phone, checked my messages, or even opened my computer for that matter. It has been forty-eight hours of Cheetos, Diet Coke and nineties rom-coms.

"Up and at 'em!" Isabella and Kenzie charge through my door like a herd of wild animals.

"I don't wanna." I pull the covers up over my head.

"Too bad. One, you're starting to stink up the place," Bella starts.

"And two, we have lots of shopping to do," Kenzie finishes.

"Shopping? For what?" I peek my head out.

"Have you forgotten that we leave in ten days for Michael and Jessi's wedding weekend?"

Holy shit. How did I forget about this? I'm going to go down as one of the worst bridesmaids in history. I have been so self-absorbed in my own drama; I've completely forgotten about my friends.

"Give me an hour. Some retail therapy may be just what I need."

Knowing we're about to do some damage, we hop into Isabella's SUV and make our way to South Coast Plaza.

"All right, here are all the events, so we can best plan out what we need."

"Ah, Kenz, our little Type A planner. What would we do without you?" Bella teases.

"Be lost in a mindless world of shopping," she snaps back.

"Doesn't sound so bad to me, but I'm glad we have your guidance, Kenzie. So, tell, oh wise planner, what do we need for the wedding extravaganza?"

Ignoring our teasing, she reads off her list. "The rehearsal dinner, girls' brunch, and the after party."

"Piece of cake! Hopefully, our bank accounts can handle it."

We hit Stella McCartney, Oscar de la Renta, and Chanel before lunch to make sure we can slip into those amazing dresses before we stuff ourselves with the most mouth-watering sushi in southern California.

"All right, girlfriend. We ordered our tea, now it's time for you to spill yours. What the hell is going on with you? Are you and Bennett having problems?"

"Not necessarily Bennett and me, as it is just me. *I'm* having problems." I hide my face in my hands, embarrassed I haven't been able to figure this out on my own.

"Oh, honey. Talk to us. You know we are always here for you. No matter what." Kenzie wraps her arm around my shoulder.

"When I watched Bennett kiss Emily Buchman, it made me uncomfortable. I know they're acting, but after seeing it in person, it grossed me out. I didn't want to kiss him for the rest of the day."

"You've seen him kiss other women before. We've been watching him on television for years. We've always said the way he kisses is one of the sexiest things about him," Bella says.

"Exactly. I agree when it's Bennett the TV star, but when it's Bennett, my boyfriend, it's awkward. I'm having difficulty separating the two."

"I'm not sure I'd be okay with my boyfriend going to work every day, knowing he's kissing and sometimes even in bed with other women," Bella says.

"But then I remember, I'm Bennett Blakely's girlfriend. I'm the one he chooses to come home to at night."

"When he comes home. You're sitting home alone more nights than you ever did before because you're waiting for his call from some remote location in Canada."

"Damn, Bella. I thought you liked Bennett," I say.

"I do, but lately you just don't seem very happy. I just wonder if Bennett is the man of your dreams or the man in your fantasies. Is he willing to sacrifice things to make you happy?"

"Bennett told me he loved me," I confess.

"He did? When? Did you say it back? And how come we are just now hearing about this?" Kenzie hits me with a ton of questions all at once.

"On the way to Mandi's baby shower, right after I watched the adlibbed kiss from Emily. I told him how uncomfortable the situation made me, he told me he loved me."

"Did you say it back?" Bella asks.

"I couldn't. Something inside just… stopped me. We spent the next two days in Santa Barbara like nothing happened. Neither one of us has brought it up again."

"Do you think kissing Adam is messing with your head?"

"It's definitely not helping. We went out the other night and had way too much to drink. He kissed me again."

"What did you do?"

"Same thing I always do when it comes to having any feelings for Adam. I run. People fall out of love too easily nowadays. After a relationship has run its course, people leave. If Adam and I don't have a relationship, he can't leave me."

"You know how stupid that sounds, right?" Bella shoots it to me straight. "Not all relationships are like your fathers. If two people truly love each other, love will never run its course."

"I need shoes. Does anyone else need shoes?" I ask with an obvious change of subject. "Stupidly, expensive red-bottomed shoes will make me feel much better right now.

My head has been a jumbled mess for the past week. Luckily, Adam has been working doubles at the hospital and Bennett has had long days on the set and I've been able to avoid them both.

The first kiss with Adam was done on a dare, but damn if it didn't make my toes curl. The second kiss took me off guard, but I liked it. Almost too much. If I hadn't pushed him away, I knew it could have gone too far. Could I be falling for Adam?

No matter how I'm feeling, I need to tell Bennett what happened the other night with Adam. He's asked a few times this week why I was avoiding him and to let him fix whatever is wrong. The thing is, I don't think it's a problem he can fix.

My phone vibrates with an incoming text.

Bennett: *Hi, sweet lips. I miss you terribly. You up for dinner and drinks tonight? Just the two of us. xoxo*

Me: *I'd like that. Pick me up in an hour.*

Like the true gentleman he is, Bennett shows up ten minutes early, with a dozen roses in hand. "You look gorgeous."

He pulls me into a kiss, but something is off. It feels forced. A strange sense of guilt washes over me, but for what and to whom, I'm not sure.

"So do you," I say, pushing back.

"Ready? I have a fun evening planned. He might not want to continue this evening very long after he hears my confession.

"Thanks for inviting me to dinner," I say, as his car speeds down Pacific Coast Highway.

"I would have taken you to dinner every night this week if I could have."

"I know. I'm sorry. With the wedding coming up and being gone for another week, I've been trying to get my loose ends tied up."

"The nice thing about traveling all the time is my loose ends come with me. So, when they called me yesterday and asked if I could leave a month early for the Costa Rica shoot, I was like no problemo."

"When do you leave?"

"This Wednesday. I'll be lost in a tropical jungle for three weeks."

"What about Hope's Landing? How does that work with your schedule here?"

"We film so far in advance; they can change what happens to my character. He'll either be kidnapped or go on vacation."

"Do you ever think about slowing down?" I ask.

"No. Why would I? I have the greatest job in the world."

Not knowing how to respond, I welcome the interruption of a baby's cry coming through the speakers. Bennett looks confused, and almost a bit annoyed. His car's Bluetooth must still be connected to my phone after the last time we drove it.

"It's Mandi's ringtone. I wanted something distinctive so I won't miss her calls. Hey little momma. What's up?" I answer.

"Hey, big sister. Whatcha doin'?"

"Uh oh. You only call me big sister when you want something. What's up?"

"Pottery Barn just called and they finally have the bouncer I've been wanting in stock. But only at the Newport Beach store, which is like a three hour round trip for me. Is there any way you can pick it for us? Please?"

"I'm going out to dinner with Bennett. Can I get it in the morning?"

"They usually sell out in a few hours because they are the hottest new Hollywood baby item. Can you pleeeeease do it tonight?"

"We gotcha covered, Mandi. Uncle Bennett to the rescue."

Walking through the shopping center with Bennett is proving more challenging than I anticipated. Strangers constantly stop him for autographs or pictures and a few have even asked for a kiss.

Bennett thrives on being the center of attention. When he's surrounded by fans his eyes sparkle with a happiness I remember seeing in my mother. His face lights up the entire room as these ladies tell him the best part of their day is when Ryan Hope graces their screen for an hour.

Not wanting to be a part of Bennett's fanfare, I slowly back my way out of the crowd and into the Pottery Barn behind us. Watching from the store entrance, dozens of thirsty women surround him. Between the signing and the pictures, I'm not sure he even notices I'm not by his side anymore.

Wandering up and down the baby aisles, I pick out the few things Mandi mentioned they still needed before Tallulah makes her arrival next month.

"Hey, stranger." Bennett comes up behind me sliding his arms around my waist. "I thought I lost you."

"Nope. I'm just not a huge fan of crowds of people surrounding me. Brings back memories sometimes I wish I could forget."

"I'm sorry, sweet lips. I didn't even think about it. Let's pay for these things and get to dinner."

"Thanks."

Bennett's jaw drops when the cashier rings up my items. "Is this seat really almost three hundred dollars? For that kind of money, it better wipe the baby's butt and change her diaper too."

"No, it's just a bouncy seat." I chuckle.

"Damn, kids are expensive." I can't tell if he's being sarcastic or if he's serious.

"It's a good thing you have money," I tease.

"It's a good thing I don't want kids."

I guess he was serious.

Pulling into Bennett's driveway, I'm confused by where we are. "I thought we were going to dinner?"

"After the incident at Pottery Barn, I thought we needed some privacy so I thought I'd have dinner delivered and we could talk about whatever has been bothering you lately."

"Okay."

Bennett pours us each a glass of wine; I grab a blanket and we make our way to the sand to watch the sunset. We sit silently, watching the sky change from a vivid clear blue to brilliant shades of pink and orange. I know Bennett is waiting for me to start but the knots in my stomach are preventing words from forming in my mouth.

"Johana, please tell me what's going on. You're starting to scare me. Before we left for Kauai, I felt like our relationship was on such a high. It wasn't easy for me to tell you I love you. I keep waiting to hear you say it and each day you don't I worry you don't feel the same way for me as I do about you."

"Adam and I kissed."

"I know. It was a dare. I was there."

"We kissed again the other night. We went out to make up from our fight and talk about his break-up with Breeann and he kissed me," I confess.

"I always knew Adam wanted you. Perfect ploy. Fake the best friend game until you get into the girl's pants."

"Adam has faked anything a day in his life. He has been my best friend since the day I met him and he has never once tried to get in my pants." That's not entirely true, but in Adam's defense he was just trying to fulfill a pact I made.

"Why do you think he kissed you?" Bennett's voice catches as he asks his question.

"I don't know, maybe because we were drunk. Maybe because he was upset after his break-up. I didn't stick around long enough to find out. I called Kenzie to come get me and I haven't talked to him since."

"Let's keep it that way because I do not like the idea of this guy thinking it's okay to kiss my girlfriend."

If there is anything that can piss me off it's someone thinking they have the right to tell me what I can and cannot do. Especially when it comes to Adam.

"I feel the same way about Emily."

"What are you talking about? Kissing Emily is part of my job. We are acting."

"You may be, but is she? It was a perfectly timed kiss when your girlfriend was on the set. I watched you kiss Emily the same way you kiss me, I didn't like it. Honestly, I had a difficult time kissing you the rest of the day. It was the first time I was unable to separate Bennett, the actor, from Bennett, my boyfriend. When you go to work, your job is to make millions of women fall in love with your captivating personality and sexy smile. To me, kisses are intimate and personal and I don't know if I'm the woman who is willing to share my man with the world."

"I'm sorry you feel that way, Johana, but that's my career. My livelihood, my passion."

"I know and I'd never ask you to give up your dreams. Do you want kids?" I ask.

"No. I love my life of being able to do what I want when I want."

"I want three. Two boys and a girl. And maybe be fortunate enough to adopt a fourth."

"Johana, if kids are what you want, we can work something out."

"Work something out? Seriously? I want to love a man who's going to be a dad because he wants to be, not because I forced him to be."

"Sweet lips, we don't know what the future holds. Maybe in a few years we will both change what we want. People change all the time for love."

"But that's just it, we shouldn't have to change. The one thing you love the most is the one thing I can never love again. Hollywood took my mother from me. I would never want to put my children through the same heartache I felt. Our dinner in Kauai was an eye-opener, but today scared me. Scared is not how I want to live."

"What happened to your mother was a tragic accident. It doesn't mean it will happen to us."

"Bennett, I need you to understand it's more than just what happened to my mother. It's the weeks alone while you're off shooting somewhere. Or knowing when you go to work, your job entails kissing other women. When we first started dating, I was swept up in the fantasy of dating *the* Bennett Blakely, but the reality is, I'm not cut out to be a Hollywood wife. I don't think I can be your girlfriend anymore."

Tears flow freely down both our faces. Even if we aren't right for each other in the future, what we had was real. "I had no idea you were feeling this way. I never dreamed we'd be having this conversation. I thought we'd be the couple to ride off into the Hollywood sunset together."

"I'm so sorry." My words muffled through heavy sobs.

"Come here." Bennett pulls me onto his lap, wiping my tears away with the pads of thumbs. "Don't be sorry, sweet lips. I'm not. Being with you the last few months has been some of the most unforgettable times of my life. I wouldn't change a single moment. Sometimes love just isn't enough to keep two people together. You deserve someone who will give you everything you've ever dreamed of."

"I do love you," I whisper, curling into his strong chest. Bennett kisses the top of my head, squeezing me just a little bit tighter.

We sit in silence until the sun sets over the horizon. "Come on. Let me take you home."

Chapter Twenty-Two

Adam

With being a nurse, I find myself comfortable in most situations. Not much bothers me, but awkward silence is something I can't handle. The seven-hour drive to San Francisco is going to be excruciating if Joey and I can't resolve whatever is going between us.

Johana and I haven't spoken since the night we kissed and yet Bella had the brilliant idea to stick us in a car together. Alone. For seven hours.

"I'm excited for Michael and Jessi. They're good people," I say in a feeble attempt to break the silence.

"Yeah, it should be a fun weekend." Johana goes right back to staring out the window.

Thirty minutes pass without another word. "This is going to be a really long weekend if we don't talk to each other. I'm sorry for kissing you. I way overstepped my boundaries with you. It won't ever happen again. I'll talk to Bennett and smooth things over."

"Bennett and I broke up," she says with no emotion in her voice. I wait for an explanation but nothing follows.

Needing a leg stretch and food we stop in Santa Nella for a break. I immediately text Bella.

Me: *Did you know Joey and Bennett broke up?*

Bella: *No! When the hell did that happen?*

Me: *I have no idea. She has barely said two words to me for the entire drive.*

Bella: *When Jo gets back from the bathroom, send her to ride with me. We need to get to the bottom of this.*

For the next three hours, I overanalyze Joey's four simple words. Bennett and I broke up. Why did they break up? Was it because of our kiss? Who broke up with who? Does this mean I should make my move? Should I just be the best friend who supports her through it? Could I end up being the rebound guy?

Arriving at the San Francisco Four Seasons, the ladies are already in line for us to check-in. "Damn. This place is nice. Glad I don't have to pay for it," I tease.

"You're such a cheapskate!" Bella playfully slaps my chest.

"No, I'm practical. Five hundred a night is insane. The bed here is the same as the bed at Best Western down the street."

"You really didn't just say that did you?" Joey says, face cringed.

"Welcome to the Four Seasons San Francisco. Checking in?"

"Yes. We are with the Barcon wedding party. Our rooms should be booked under Crawford and Russo," Bella tells her.

"I see here Miss Russo is booked for one deluxe room with two queen beds. And Mr. Crawford, you are staying in our king deluxe suite."

"Lucky you," Kenzie teases. "Perks of being the best man."

"King suite?" Joey questions. "There's only one bed?"

"Yes, ma'am, but there is a couch bed."

"Oh, okay." Why does Joey look so worried? Is she afraid to be around me?

"Michael didn't tell me about a room upgrade," I whisper to Bella while walking to the elevator.

"You can pay me back later." She winks as we pack in the elevator with our overabundance of luggage.

"What's on the agenda for tonight?" I ask.

"Nothing for the wedding until tomorrow, so I thought we could have some fun in the city. I absolutely love San Francisco. If Johana hadn't asked me to move in with her, this is probably where I would have ended up."

"Sounds like fun. We spent so much time up here when we were in college. You up for its Johana?" Kenzie asks.

"Definitely. A night out with my best friends is exactly what I need."

The one room suite has a breathtaking view overlooking the city and the San Francisco Bay. We can see from the Golden Gate Bridge to the Bay Bridge with everything in between. I take Joey's luggage to the bedroom first and then find a place for mine next to the couch, where—apparently—I'll be sleeping.

"Are you sure the couch is going to be okay?" she asks.

"Well, it isn't the Best Western but I think I'll survive." I laugh. "Any idea what Bella has up her sleeve for tonight?"

"Knowing Bella in San Fran, we could be in for one hell of a night. I'm gonna go hop in the shower and freshen up."

I use the few minutes of alone time to text Bella.

Me: *Anything I need to know for tonight?*

Bella: *Nope. Leave it all up to me.*

Me: *What do you have up your sleeve?*

Bella: *Just you wait and see. Meet us in the lobby at seven.*

I grab the bottle of Grey Goose along with some cranberry juice from the mini bar. I pour Joey's first. I knock on the bathroom door.

"Yeah?"

"Is it unlocked?"

"Yeah. Do you need something?"

You. I need you. But of course, I can't tell her. "I have something for you." Opening the door only enough for my hand to fit in, I place the drink on the counter for her.

Twenty minutes later, Joey emerges from the bathroom, wrapped in the plush robes provided by the hotel. Her hair is wrapped in one of those twisty towel things. And not one ounce of make-up on her skin. She has never looked more beautiful.

"I'm not sure what's better, the shower, the robe or this drink?" She sits next to me on the couch.

"My vote would be for the company," I tease.

She rests her head on my shoulder. "I definitely like my company."

"You ready to talk about it?"

"The kiss or the break-up?"

"Either."

"After that night on the beach, I secluded myself from everyone for days. I needed to clear my head. I knew I needed to tell him about our second kiss and when I did, he told me to stay away from you."

"Like hell you will."

"I know, it's okay. Me breaking up with Bennett wasn't about our kiss. He and I just want two different things from life. He wants fame and fortune and I want the white picket fence with a bunch of kids running through the yard."

"How did he take it?" I ask.

"Not good. But ultimately, we realized we weren't right for each other."

"And the kiss?" I push my luck.

"Not yet."

"Fair enough. Now go get ready. We meet the girls in the lobby in an hour and we know

how Bella gets if we're not on time."

"Thanks." She leans over and kisses my cheek before jumping up to finish getting dressed.

"First order of business is dinner and drinks. The Uber will be here in five minutes," Bella informs us when we enter the lobby.

"And after that?" Joey asks.

"That's for me to know and you to find out."

"Uh-oh." She laughs.

"Don't worry. I'm sure Superman over here will keep you nice and protected." Bella smacks me on the back.

"Stop! Who are you and what did you do with my friend Isabella? Did you actually just give Adam a compliment?" Joey teases.

"What can I say? The guy's growing on me."

"Only took you ten years," I quip.

"Stop, children," Kenzie interrupts. "Our ride is here."

Our first stop is at Fisherman's Wharf for sidewalk street food. For some reason, the crab always tastes better from a street vendor eaten on a curb overlooking the bay. I crack a leg sending meat flying everywhere causing contagious laughter between us all.

"Damn, I've missed this," says Bella, eating her shrimp po' boy.

"Would you have really moved up here if I hadn't asked you to come live with me?" Joey asks.

"Definitely. I could see myself opening up an edgy boutique somewhere downtown. Maybe one day." She sighs.

"What? So, you're just gonna ditch our little trio here?" Kenzie teases.

"Eventually, we all have to grow up and move one, little one." Bella playfully pats Kenzie on her head.

"Nope. I refuse to accept that." She laughs.

"Alright people! Finish up! We have a schedule to keep," Bella announces.

"Seriously? There's an itinerary for our night of fun?" Joey asks.

"There is. We only have one night of freedom in this amazing city! We've got places to go and people to see."

"People to see?"

"You heard me. Now finish up," she demands.

Within minutes, we scarfed down the remainder of our food and were swept away by another Uber. During the twenty-minute ride, I listen to the girls go on and on about the amazing times they had in the city during college. They talk about the bars they went to, concerts they saw, and all the fun and crazy people they met along the way. If Joey and I had been together, she would have missed out on all those experiences that make her the amazing person she is today.

As we pull up to the bar, the screech from the backseat nearly pierces my eardrums. I'm not sure I've ever seen the three of them so excited for anything before.

"What is this place?" I ask the driver.

"Karaoke bar. Best in town."

Karaoke? Oh, hell no. I do not sing.

"Pandora!" Joey shouts. "Please tell me you booked our favorite room."

"Um, would we party any other way?" The happiness of these three is contagious. As much as I hate karaoke, I don't think I cannot have fun tonight.

"All right, people we got two hours until our next destination."

"There's more?" Joey asks. Bella's only response is a wink.

Bella walks to the front like she owns the place. "Russo's Roosters, party of 4," she tells the bouncer.

He looks up from his clipboard, "Isabella? Little Bella Russo, is that you?"

"Uncle Vinnie? You're still here? How are you?"

"Of course, I'm still here. They pay me too good to leave. Plus, I own the joint now," he whispers like it's a secret. "No fricken' way! Are you three still causing raucous together? Jo, Kenzie get your asses over here and give your uncle a hug."

Here I stand, like an awkward fish out of water. "Which one of you got your man over there looking all helpless and alone?"

"Vinnie, this is my best friend, Adam. Adam, this is Uncle Vinnie."

"*The* Adam? The Adam, you used to go on and on about after you had too much to drink?"

"Excuse me?" My eyebrow raises in question, but there is an undeniable smile plastered across my face.

"I knew the girls were giving me fake IDs to get in, so in return for me not ratting them out they stayed after closing and helped me clean up. It was a win-win for all of us."

Even in the dark glow of the outside club lights, Joey's cheeks turn the sexiest shade of pink.

"Now that Jo has had her embarrassment for the evening, I think it's time for the rest of us to do the same. To the Bat Cave Roosters!" Bella shouts, opening the doors to the club.

"Welcome back, Roosters. Enjoy yourself. The night is on me," Uncle Vinnie says, waving us off.

"Roosters?" I ask.

"It was our karaoke group name. Don't ask." Joey laughs.

The girls link hands as they push their way through the crowded main bar to get to our reserved room. Upon opening the door to the Bat Cave, I entered every comic book nerd's wet dream. Batman and Robin are kissing on the wall in front of me. Wonder Woman is licking her microphone and Green Ivy is really feeling the ganja.

"Holy shit. This is the room you girls choose to party in?"

"Johana used to make the reservations and this was always the room we ended up with,"

Kenzie explains. "Though she swears she's not into comic books." But I am. Joey would pretend to hate them but I'd always catch reading them.

"Really now?" I smile but won't give away her secret.

"Oh, looky here. There's already a bottle waiting for us." Joey pulls Bella and Kenzie to the mics avoiding any further comic book conversation.

I pour us each a shot of Grey Goose Vodka. "Toast. Here's to old friends and new beginnings."

"Cheers." We all clink and drink. The girls do two more while getting ready to sing what they call their song.

I settle into the oversized couch after pouring myself a larger glass of vodka. The music starts and I vaguely recognize the beat. As soon as they start singing about humps and lumps, I know exactly where this is going.

Their singing is atrocious but the bumping and grinding of their lovely lady lumps is quite entertaining. Behind her back, Bella motions to me to join them. I pretend not to see her, guzzling my glass of vodka.

"You ready to sing, Adam?"

"Nope. There's enough vodka in this club to get me to sing karaoke. You guys do another. I will sit here and enjoy my drink."

The girls sing Unwritten, Girls Just Wanna Have Fun, and Hot in Here, begging me to join them in between each song. Each time, I decline continuing to drink the bottle of vodka by myself.

"This is much more exhausting than I remember," Joey says, plopping down on the couch next to me, stealing the drink from my hand.

"We're also ten years older," Kenzie adds.

"Don't remind me," she groans.

"I'm ready." I bounce up from the couch unexpectedly, scaring everyone. Liquid courage is making me believe I can sing.

I shuffle through the playlist, praying I can find the one song I've decided to sing. Found it.

"Thinking out Loud" by Ed Sheeran.

Here goes nothing.

Chapter Twenty-Three

Johana

Adam's hand shakes as he scrolls through the playlist on the tablet. For as long as I've known Adam, he's never done karaoke. He swears he has the worst voice, but I've yet to hear it. Even when I sing in the car, he hums along quietly.

"Do you want a partner?" Bella asks.

"Nope." His voice cracks and I am worried for him.

Adam presses play, with a death grip on the microphone. The music starts and his whole body starts to shake.

"You got this," I mouth to him. Our eyes lock and he doesn't look away as he starts singing.

Tears swell my eyes when he sings the few lines of "Thinking Out Loud" by Ed Sheeran. Adam's voice is magnificent. Throughout the song, our eye contact never breaks. My body covers in goosebumps as he hits each note perfectly. His voice is smooth and silky and completely turns me on.

"You knew all the words by heart."

"I've been practicing." He laughs.

"For a random karaoke night in San Francisco?" I joke, deflecting anything serious.

"Not necessarily. Just waiting for the right moment to sing it to you. Do you remember the first time we heard it?"

"Kenzie twenty-first birthday party in Half Moon Bay. I was being stalked by that crazy guy-"

"That was my brother and he was fifteen," Kenzie interjects.

"Any who, we were hiding out in your truck from the hormone crazed teenager getting drunk. This song came on the radio and I replayed it over and over again, until I memorized every word. I was obsessed with Ed Sheeran that summer."

"I also memorized every word because that song tells our story or what I want our story to be."

"Bella, don't we have to get to the next spot? It's already ten-thirty."

"You can't keep changing the subject, Johana. We have to talk about this."

"Oh, we will. Just not while you're drunk in a karaoke bar."

Pulling up to our third stop of the evening, my heart stops. No, no, no. I did this once with Isabella, I don't want to do it again.

"Seriously? Is this the same Madame Celeste? Didn't we learn last time that her reading was a joke?"

"This is about me, not you. So just indulge me, please. It's been five years since I've had my cards read. She knows things. Now, come on before we're late."

"Welcome. Welcome," Madame Celeste greets us as we enter her tiny room. "Isabella, we have a card reading tonight. Please take a seat at my table. The rest of you can wait over there until it's your turn." She points to a long booth at the other end of the room. Confused and afraid to argue with the old lady, we do as we're told.

All through Bella's reading, Madame Celeste keeps looking at us like we're trying to steal something. "I'm sorry, Isabella. We need to stop. There is just too much noise in here right now."

"We haven't said a word," I whisper to Adam.

"Any of you have a relative who has passed starting with the letter C?" Madame Celeste asks. "She's loud and a little hard to understand."

"My mother's name was Charlotte. She was Australian."

"Does a baby kangaroo mean anything to you?"

"She called me her joey."

"Please come sit." Madame Celeste directs me to her table. "I have a feeling if I don't help this one talk, she may haunt me forever."

The old woman takes her hands in mine and closes her eyes. Frankly, I'm a bit creeped out by it all.

"First, your mother says she's proud of the woman you have become. She wishes she could have been there for you. She also wants you to stop putting a wall up around your heart. Trust who the universe has put in front of you."

I pull my hands back from hers. "This all sounds like a bunch of generic bull crap my friends over there have fed you to get me to believe

I'm supposed to fall in love with Adam. You guys are so obvious. It's sad. I thought you we're going to try to bring up the true love reading, but instead you bring up my dead mother."

"That's where I recognize you from." Madame Celeste jumps from her chair pointing at me. "You had a reading with me seven years ago that changed my life. Your mother was the first ghost I ever communicated with. I didn't say anything at the time, because it had never happened before and I just thought I had finally gone bat-shit crazy. Your mother opened up an entire new realm for me."

"You guys took this a little over the top, don't you think?"

"Jo, I'll admit I may have manipulated a few things this weekend to push you and Adam together, but this was supposed to be a card reading. I would never play around with the memory of your mother," Bella says.

"If my mother really is here, have her tell you something only she and I know about."

"She says when you were five, she used to take you to ride the carousel in Central Park."

"We did, but I have a picture of that in my living room."

"Lullaby and Goodnight was your favorite story for me to read each night."

"It's the most popular bedtime story read in Australia."

"She says she knows why Adam is the only one you allow to call you Joey."

"Excuse me?" If my jaw could have hit the floor it would have. The gasp from my friends is loud enough for me to hear from across the room.

"Wait. She's never told you either?" Bella asks Adam. He shakes his head.

"She wants to know if you saw her with you the day you met Adam?" Madame Celeste asks.

"Once. When the teacher directed me to sit next to Adam, she was standing behind him, smiling. It was the first time I had ever seen a ghost, no less hers, and I thought it was something I created in my imagination."

"She wanted you to know Adam was your safe place. Amongst all the noise, he is your calm."

"This can't be… I mean, how?" I stammer, unable to complete a thought.

"Just trust in the universe, darling," Madame Celeste says in a reassuring voice. "And it's quiet again."

"Wait, she's gone? I had more to say." Tears flood my eyes.

"Talk to her anytime. She's always listening."

I haven't said a word since we left Madame Celeste's. The past week has been this insane roller coaster of emotions that has finally come to a screeching halt. Between Adam, Bennett, and now my mother, I don't know what's up from down anymore.

Falling down on the bed, I hug my pillow tightly and start to cry. "Can I get you anything?" Adam asks.

"Just hold me until I fall asleep, please."

"Of course." He wraps his body around mine. The strength of his arms wrapped around me brings me comfort. "I got you, Joey. Now and forever. I've got you."

My body relaxes into his and I quickly drift off to sleep.

"Places, everyone. Places." The wedding coordinator has us lined up in the order we are to walk down the aisle.

I woke up this morning happy and refreshed, like an invisible weight was lifted off my shoulders. I can't explain it. It just feels like everything is right with the universe.

The doors open and the first couple make their way down the aisle with their fun choreographed dance to Bruno Mars' "I Think I Want to Marry You". I'm third to go paired up with Michael's friend Max, who is a complete goofball. Adam is last, paired with Jessi's sister Suzanne. His dance moves are almost as impressive as his singing.

When Jessi makes her entrance, all eyes turn to her, but I can't take my eyes off Adam. He is the most gorgeous man in this entire room. He has the biggest heart. How have I been so blind? Adam's my penguin.

The ceremony, the pictures and all bridal party duties seem to drag on forever when all I want is five minutes alone with Adam. As we're eating dinner, he looks down the table, catching me staring at him. He nods his head toward the terrace and my feet can get me outside quick enough.

"Hi."

"Hi." Adam and I stand inches apart. My palms are sweaty, my mouth is dry, and it feels like my heart is trying to escape from my chest.

"Moon River" echoes from inside. "Can I have this dance?" he asks.

I wrap my arms around his neck, pulling us close together. Faces connected; we dance in silence.

I bring my lips to his. I start slow, scared he may push me away after all the times I've done it to him. Instead, his strong hands cup my face and our kiss deepens. Our tongues wrestle for control of the most delicious thing they've ever tasted.

Needing to come up for air, I pull away, gently biting his lip as we separate.

"Wow."

"Wow." Adam's smile is infectious. As cold as it is on this San Francisco evening, every part of my body is basking in his glow. "Does this mean…?" His question trails off.

"I love you, Adam Crawford. I love you so fucking much."

"I love you, too, Joey. I've loved you since the day we met and I promise you I will love you for the rest of my life. You are my penguin, baby. I'm never letting you go again."

Adam pulls me in for another kiss, holding me tighter than he ever has before. "Is that your phone or are you just that excited to kiss me?" I tease.

"Both." He laughs. "It's my mom."

"Answer it."

"Hello? What? Slow down. I can't understand you. What's going on?" The pause of not being able to hear her response is killing me. "Okay. Yeah, she's here with me now. We're on our way."

"Come on. We gotta go. Mandi's in labor. It's too early. She's not due for another few weeks."

"Calm down. Three weeks is not that early. Let's go say goodbye, get our stuff and get out of here. Your niece is going to be beautiful and perfect and I can't wait to meet her."

Adam and I are like a well-oiled machine. We make the rounds and say goodbye to the people we need to, change, pack, and are on the road in less than thirty minutes.

"*Our* niece. Tallulah is *our* niece," Adam says out of nowhere, thirty minutes into our drive.

"Tallulah's father is my ex-stepbrother. Again, that doesn't qualify me as her aunt."

"You don't get it, do you? You know the twins still call you their big sister, right?"

I shake my head no.

"They've never put an *ex* or a *step* in front of it. Do you know why my mom asked if you were with me?"

"No."

"Because Mandi called you before anyone else. She looks up to you like the big sister she always wanted. I mean, of course, I'm an awesome big brother, but I'm chopped liver compared to you."

"Really?"

"Really," he reassures me.

"When my mother died, I felt like my family died with her. After that, I always felt like an outsider looking in. Like I never belonged anywhere. My father seamlessly took over the father-figure role of the twins, but Crystal never once tried to act like my mother."

"You never let her, Joey. I'm not saying Crystal ever would have acted like a mom, but you had your walls up so high. She never had a chance. Let your walls down. You may realize the people you've been running from are the best family you could ever want. And you are going to make a terrific aunt to our little niece."

I lean over, resting my head on Adam's shoulder. He kisses my forehead. "I guess I need to just trust the universe."

We arrive at Mandi and Linc's home in Santa Barbara just before five in the morning, missing Tallulah's birth by forty-five minutes. She's already just like her auntie, early and eager to get life going.

My brother, Linc, my father and Mr. Crawford are outside smoking cigars. "Congratulations, Dad and grandpas." I hug all three.

"You better get in there. Mandi has been asking for you for hours."

Walking in, both Crystal and Annie hug me and point me to the back room where Mandi is recovering. Something's weird. Everyone's vibe seems off.

"Hey, beautiful mama. How are you?" I ask, quietly entering her room.

"I'm amazing. Look at how pretty she is." She turns the bassinet towards me.

"She's perfect. She looks just like you. I'm so sorry I wasn't here for you today."

"You're here now and that's all that matters. Thank you for always being my big sister," she says.

"Okay. What is going on? Why is everyone acting so strange?" I ask.

"So, first off, I didn't know anything about this until Crystal came to visit two weeks ago. I wanted to talk to you about it as soon as I found out, but then you weren't answering your calls or texts and then you left for the wedding. Then, Tally came early."

"Mandi, what are you talking about?"

"Go look at the back wall in Tally's room."

Opening the door to the nursery, I gasp loud enough to cause Adam to come running from the next room.

"What the hell? How can this be?" I look to Adam for answers.

He shrugs. "I'm not the person to ask."

"Mandi, where did you get those?" I ask, running back down the hall.

"Okay, so my friends and I were outside riding our bikes and the new neighbor lady dragged a box to the curb and wrote charity on it. We thought there was some cool stuff in it so we carried it over to my garage and took what we wanted. About an hour later, a guy with a charity sticker on his van asked if we had seen a box he was supposed to pick up. Being six years old we hid the box and never spoke about it again because we didn't want to get in trouble."

"You must have hidden it well because Dad and I cleaned out the garage many times over the years," Adam says.

"Not really. I just wrote girly things on it and you two never touched it. Johana, Crystal told me those are the antique snow globes your mother gave you."

"They are. I thought I'd never see them again." The tears running down my face are a fucked-up mix of being happy, sad, and just completely overwhelmed. I bury my head in Adam's chest and cry. The kiss on the top of the head lets me know he's got me.

"Wait? Are you two—?"

Adam shushes his sister's question.

"Johana, we're going to get them all taken down and given back to you."

"Don't you dare." I pull away from Adam and sit next to her on the bed. "I learned this weekend the universe has a funny way of making everything come together the way it's supposed to. You saved my snow globes. You have no idea what you've done for me. So, for now, the globes will look after my niece, the same way they did for me. Hopefully, one day you'll be able to pass them along and they'll be able to watch over my children."

"I promise you they will always be in our family." She squeezes my hands and for the first time in twenty years I know I'm with family.

Adam and I pull up to my condo the following afternoon. He turns off the engine and we just sit and stare at each other, neither of us knowing what happens next.

"What a weekend."

"What a weekend." I laugh. "How much of this weekend was real and how much was set up by Bella?"

"Every bit of it was real. Bella just nudged us in the right direction."

"So… Now what?" I ask.

"Miss Johana Warner, will you go on a date with me?"

I crawl over the center console of the Jeep, straddling Adam's lap. "I thought you'd never ask." A smirk creeps from the corners of my lips.

"What am I going to do with you?" Adam laughs, shaking his head.

"Just love me. From now until forever, just love me."

Adam pushes my hair behind my ear. "Easiest thing I've ever done in my life." His mouth takes control of mine and I surrender, finally giving him every piece of my heart.

Chapter Twenty-Four

Johana
Six Months Later

"Adam! You're home. All right, everybody, time to eat." Tonight, I'm hosting our first family Christmas Eve dinner. Our home is filled with family, friends, and anyone else who needs a place to spend Christmas Eve.

I grab Adam's hand and pull him into our bedroom. I push him up against the closed door causing a thud I'm sure the whole house heard. "Do you know how sexy you are in your scrubs?" I slide my hand down his pants and run my nails along his growing shaft.

"I thought you didn't like my scrubs. And we have a house full of our family in the next room. We need to get back out there."

"They'll never know. We can be quick. If you loved me, you'd so it." She giggles.

"Baby, I love you but I am not having a quickie with your dad in the next room. What has gotten into you?"

I shake my head. "You always have been the goody two-shoes in this relationship."

"I'll show you how goody two-shoes I am later when I'm paddling that ass of yours for getting me all turned on before dinner with our parents."

"Promises, promises." I giggle before kissing him and bouncing out of our room leaving Adam to clean up after work.

"Why are you in a suit?" I ask, handing Adam a beer. He grabs my hand before I can walk away.

"Everybody, can I have your attention, please? I want to thank you all for coming tonight to celebrate Christmas with Joey and I in our new home. As some may say, the universe has presented us with many blessings this year. I want to keep creating blessings and miracles with you all for the rest of my life. Especially you." He gives me a sweet kiss.

The room erupts in cheers.

"Blindfold." he says boldly, catching me off guard.

"I thought you didn't want to act like this in front of our guests," I tease.

"Careful, little girl, Santa may put you on the naughty list."

"Watch it. Dad in the room," my dad yells from the living room.

Bella covers my eyes and leads me out front. "You're in on this?" I ask.

"Of course I am. We both know Adam can't pull things off without me."

She guides me down the stairs and onto the front lawn before removing the blindfold. Adam is standing with Santa Claus inside a ten-foot inflatable snow globe on my front lawn. Someone dressed as an elf grabs my hand and leads into the snow globe with them. Santa hands Adam a box and leaves.

"Adam, what's going on?" I ask.

He gets down on one knee and takes my hand. "Johana Warner, you are my best friend. The love of my life. My perfect soulmate. I've known it since the day we met. You have filled my dreams, both day and night. I want to make sure every last one of your dreams is fulfilled for the rest of your life. Joey, will you make me the happiest man on earth and be my wife?"

Adam holds open a box with the most stunning princess cut solitaire diamond ring I've ever seen.

"Yes. A thousand times yes." He slides the diamond on my finger. We both fall back in the artificial snow and kiss like nobody's watching.

Bella and Kenzie stay well past midnight and help me clean up the kitchen after Adam falls asleep on the couch. "Thank you guys for helping. Adam's been exhausted after picking up extra shifts at the hospital."

"Are you going to give him your gift tonight?" Bella asks.

"I think I'll wait until tomorrow. I'm nervous."

"Oh, look, it *is* tomorrow. We know why you attacked your man as soon as he walked through the door. Now it's time to tell him."

I shut and lock the door behind my friends, turning off all the lights in the house except for the tree. I stand there for just a moment admiring its beauty.

Adam startles me as he slides his arms around my waist. "Merry Christmas, fiancée," he whispers in my ear.

"Merry Christmas, fiancé." I turn around to kiss the lips I will never get enough of.

"Did I hear you say you are nervous to give me a gift?"

"A little."

"Baby, I never want you to be nervous to tell me anything. Whatever is, we'll get through it. Together."

I link my hand in his, we walk down the hall and I open the door and turn on the light in one of the empty rooms.

"Why is one of your mom's snow globes here? I thought we were keeping them with Tally until we…" Adam stops mid-sentence as he puts the pieces together. "Are we?"

"We are. You're going to be a daddy."

Adam scoops me in his arms and swings me around. "I love you so much."

"Thank you for never giving up on me."

"I will forever be chasing you, Joey Warner."

The End

What's next?

Did you enjoy Adam and Johana's journey to happily ever after? Stay tuned for Bennett's love story in COMIN' HOME!
Pre-order your copy today!

www.books2read.com/cominhome

About the Author

Teri Kay writes contemporary romance with strong, sassy female leads and their devoted love interests.
Teri has always called Southern California home, where she lives with her husband and two small fur babies. Her first love will always be teaching, and she wouldn't want to do anything else—except maybe being a full-time writer.
Between reading, writing, and teaching, she has very little free time, but in those rare moments, you can find Teri spending time with her friends and family, binge-watching reality television show, and baking.

Follow Teri online to stay up-to-date:

Website: https://www.terikayauthor.com/
Facebook: https://www.facebook.com/terikayauthor/
Instagram: https://www.instagram.com/terikay_author/
Twitter: https://twitter.com/TeriKay_Author

Made in the USA
Middletown, DE
22 August 2022